12 Hours of Heaven

Lessons for a Better World

RICK ORNELAS

I Spark Change Media

Published by I Spark Change Media

Editor: Andrea Vanryken
Cover and Interior Design: Christy Collins
Publishing consultant: Martha Bullen

ISBN (Paperback): 978-1-7358349-0-0
ISBN (ebook): 978-1-7358349-1-7

Printed in the United States of America

Dedication

This book is dedicated to both my Heavenly Father, our Lord and Savior, and my father in Heaven, Richard "Kid" Ornelas.

First and always to GOD for giving me the motivation to write and the inspiration to let your guidance lead the story.

And to my father, Kid, who is now my Angel in Heaven. Thank you for all the lessons you taught me over your wise 96 years. You taught me most of the lessons here and gave me the greatest gifts of all: love, family and faith. I love you.

"You must love the Lord your God with all your heart, with all your soul, and with all your mind. This is the greatest and the first commandment. The second resembles it: You must love your neighbor as yourself. "
Matthew 22:37-39

CONTENTS

CHAPTER 1: THE BIG QUESTION

Heaven was ready for a change. Not the massive change that had come a millennium ago, when it was all so new to me, but a change nonetheless. Anabeth was ready for this change too. She had always been quite precocious as a young Angel-in-Training, having come to Heaven at the early age of fourteen, but this time she was ready, in the way that a toddler striving to walk is ready for the next step in life.

She is definitely my most inquisitive student, mused Ezra, with her endless questioning and incessant nature. Questioning what happens day after day … and pretty much all day long. Still, I never mind it and actually welcome it—most of the time, as she is difficult to turn down with those expressive brown eyes that sparkle like stars on her cute little cherub face that is adorned with perfectly golden Angelic hair. Yet I have always been surprised that she hasn't asked me the one question I know she constantly wonders: How did I, Ezra the Wise, become an Archangel so young and early in my tenure as an Angel?

She often hints at the question, saying things like, *"Teacher, things are far different for me than they were back when you were just an Angel-in-Training—they are a lot harder now!"* Even when I disagree, I always try to respond affirmatively with something like: "Yes, Anabeth. You're correct." It gives her the positive reinforcement she needs while keeping her inquiring and her young mind expanding.

So, it wasn't a total surprise that she would come to see me today to ask the *big* question. Well, her official reason for coming was to ask for my support in her campaign to become an Archangel, but I knew what she really wanted, despite her attempt at subterfuge. She wasn't after my support as an Angel-in-Training, this little precocious Angel who just happened to be the youngest candidate for Archangel ever, not just at her "Earth age" but in her limited time in Heaven. And she wasn't here now because of my position as her favorite teacher and mentor—although I was both those things, of course. She had approached me because I happened to be the only other Angel-in-Training to become an Archangel in the history of Heaven. And because she really wanted to know *my* story.

You see, I wasn't always Ezra, the Wisest Chief Archangel in Heaven, with my official Archangel regal-red robe, jewel-encrusted staff, and brilliant halo signifying my place amongst the Angels. Once upon a time, I was a bright-eyed and inquisitive young Angel-in-Training full of aspirations and dreams just like her, as I entered Heaven almost as young as Anabeth at the ripe old age of eighteen. And just like her, I also had the glow of youth on my light complexion, which I still retain to this day. But unlike her, I hadn't campaigned to become an Archangel. Heck, I hadn't even expected to become one at all. It all came as a bit of a surprise to me.

2

By now I've probably piqued your interest, and you want to hear the story just as badly as Anabeth. You probably want to know: How does one become an Archangel anyway? So, let me answer the *big* question for you and Anabeth. Join me as I tell you both the story of how I became the Chief Archangel, Ezra.

The Problem

"*Teacher! Teacher!*" Anabeth pressed eagerly as she persisted in interrupting my regular afternoon session in the marble meditation room—where I constantly requested that she *not* disturb me, though she never complied.

"Yes, Anabeth?" I answered.

"*Did you hear what I said? Are you going to answer?*" she insisted as she sat down on a large, white meditation pillow across from me and adjusted her light blue Angel-in-Training robe to ensure it would remain pristine.

"Okay, Okay, Anabeth." I took a big breath ...

And then I began ...

I guess you've been patient long enough. You're both correct and incorrect in what you're saying, Anabeth. Things were different back then, but they were not easier like you think. They were much more complicated. It always seemed as if the answer refused to reveal itself until the last possible second. We didn't have every solution readily available at our fingertips like you do now.

Annabeth's big brown eyes started to widen, so I knew I had her interest and she was ready to listen.

It had been many millennia since the Nine Choirs of Angels had convened an "Official Emergency Meeting," yet one was just about to begin in the Great Hall of Galilee. The hall, with its mountainous pearl pillars designed to hold up a ceiling of clouds that went on to the highest reaches of Heaven, was not used often. The events of the past few days had left everyone in Heaven with their heads spinning. St. Peter's surprise early retirement, Michael's promotion to the Pearly Gates—gates that actually sparkled with diamonds, emeralds, and rubies—and the big restructuring of upper Angel Leadership. But the big question everyone was talking about was: Who would replace Michael as the Chief Archangel? The Choirs of Angels had to decide this in just twenty-four short hours. Interestingly enough, God knew the answer to that question, yet He still tasked the Choirs with electing the next Archangel, wanting us to go through the process. It was all about us coming together to decide what was best without his help. God loved to teach us lessons back then—just as He still does with all of you today, Anabeth.

The Choirs were decidedly split, primarily between the old-school Angels, who were very traditional, and the new breed, always calling for change. It was crazy to even think we could come to a decision so quickly, but of course, God knew better. Gabriel seemed like the obvious choice, but he did so much for God already. Plus, he was old—and I mean the beginning of time kind of old. Many of his methods were outdated. He mostly practiced the kind of Old Testament rhetoric that was not too popular with the masses in those days. Many wanted to see some new life infused into our leadership. But there was a problem: No obvious choice stood out among the new breed. No clear-cut leader. Plenty of up-and-comers, certainly, but no one really stood out from the pack. We had to figure things out, and fast.

God wanted improvements and change quickly. The world was suffering, and He knew more had to be done to help His children on Earth. Of course, everything started with God and Jesus, but They knew they needed the help of their Angels to really get things done. The time had come for a new Archangel who would spearhead the change needed. An Angel like God's beloved, Raphael.

Raphael was an Archangel who didn't align with the old or the new as he related well to both, having entered Heaven near the beginning of mankind. He wasn't as well-known as Michael or Gabriel but those who knew him best knew it was the relationships he had throughout Heaven that kept him neutral. He was loved by both old and new and was known for his caring nature toward everyone, which was why God asked him to oversee everything and temporarily allowed him to wear a ceremonial purple robe only used on such special occasions. The robe served as an added visual reminder to everyone of his authority to make sure things stayed on track and that no shenanigans took place. Not that there were shenanigans back then in Heaven, but it was politics, after all, and old Earth habits die hard.

God knew that Raphael would ensure his Angels hit the twenty-four-hour deadline and followed his guidelines. He also chose Raphael for this job to exclude him from the running for Archangel. God knew that if Raphael were eligible, many would choose him as an easy way out, to avoid having to pick either side. This was definitely not God's way, as He was—and still is—never about the "easy way out." God expected us all to make the difficult choice and take the hard path, though he always allowed his Angels the freedom to journey toward their ultimate destinies by free choice and preferential love. Even in Heaven, Angels still needed this lesson reinforced. Like I said, old Earth habits die hard.

God gave Raphael only three basic rules to enforce:

1) A final decision must be made in twenty-four hours.

2) Any Angel is eligible to be chosen as the new Archangel (except for Raphael).

3) The decision had to be unanimous.

It seemed so simple—until we got to rule number three. A unanimous decision? Really? It was difficult enough getting ten or twenty of us to agree on something, but an infinite number of Angels deciding unanimously on anything? And when I say infinite, think Infinity-x, Infinity-x-Infinity-squared, or something like that, and you'll get the picture. It seemed impossible, especially when you also factored in the many different divisions of Angels: Archangels, Seraphims, Cherubims, Thrones,

Dominions, Virtues, Powers, Principalities, Guardian Angels, and Angels-in-Training (those who had not yet earned their wings)—to name the majority.

"Yep, there are a lot of us."

Yes, Anabeth, that's correct. Still, those were the rules God provided us, and so those were the rules Raphael would enforce.

The only other criteria—and this went without saying—was that all of us must adhere to the Angelic Code of Conduct. The ACOC, as it was called back then, was kind of like the Ten Commandments, but just for us Angels. It basically said that we needed to Love, Give, and Serve everyone in Heaven and on Earth in all that we did. There were some forty trillion bylaws—in fine print—that had been amended over the millennia, but they all upheld the three tenets to Love, Give, and Serve. The ACOC had grown so long that most of the Angels of the day followed them more as guidelines than rules. We all did pretty well with our fellow Heaven residents, but not so good with human beings on Earth. Only the truly pure of heart embodied the ACOC in everything he/she did with those in Heaven AND on Earth.

What made the ACOC so challenging to uphold with humans was their difficult nature. They preferred to hate than love, to take rather than give, and to cause pain and despair rather than serve. This meant it required a lot more effort and constant work on the part of all in Heaven to help set them straight. It was a monumental task that grew more daunting every day. Of course, God and Jesus did their part in the ways only they could. When things required a little more attention or took longer, they would enlist the help of one of us to let them focus on more pressing matters and speed things along.

Unfortunately, this was an imperfect system. This was what usually happened: God would decide that a human being needed help from an Angel. He would assign an Angel to the task, who would begin working with the human to the best of their ability. Things would usually start off okay until the human became stubborn and fell back into bad habits. Once the human reverted to his hardheaded ways, the Angel would grow disheartened with the whole process and not put in the effort and constant work needed. It was a vicious circle that went round and round, with little good coming out of it. In the end, most of the problems came back, and the human wound up right back where he started, with little or no change—which brings us back to the reason God wanted change in the first place. Like I said, old Earth habits are tough to break.

CHAPTER 2: LOVE, GIVE, SERVE

"*When are you going to get to the good part?*"

I could tell Anabeth was losing interest in my story as she squirmed around, sliding off the meditation pillow and nearly knocking over one of the prayer candles.

"*When do I hear how you became an Archangel?*" Anabeth pressed.

A persistent young Angel, wasn't she? I decided to give her a little more background to both teach her patience and provide more context to help her understand.

You see, Anabeth, God did not give life to His beloved children, create the world with its many blessings, and save us all from sin to watch us mess things up. He provided us all these wonderful gifts to watch us Love and Give and Serve one another. He wants us to flourish and grow in ways we can only imagine. He wants us to pass these gifts and many more on to others as we make them a part of our everyday lives. He wants us to follow the examples His Son, Jesus Christ, taught us all those years ago. That's it. Pretty simple, really, if only humans wouldn't keep letting the bad stuff get in the way. This is why these simple gifts were part of the original version of the ACOC that contained only those three words. Over the years it had grown very convoluted with all the added bylaws, but it still meant the same thing: Love, Give, Serve.

On Earth, things were convoluted, just as they were becoming with us Angels in Heaven. Humans pretended to love but were more concerned with how much love was shown to them. Humans acted like they gave by doing things such as tithing or donating to charity, only to be the first to take whatever they could for themselves. Humans served, but only in bits and pieces when convenient for them. They might bring some unwanted extra food to a homeless shelter on Thanksgiving, sure, but such slight actions all added up to a whole lot of nothing, really. A lot of wasted action leading to no results. This was the kind of thing that really frustrated God. Even more frustrating for Him was the fact that He saw it happening with all of us Angels in Heaven too. So frustrating, in fact, that He put the plan for change into action himself.

When Peter decided to retire, we Angels just assumed it was Peter's idea to do so. He had hinted about it for centuries, saying things like, "I really want to spend more time writing," or, "Being responsible for the Pearly Gates really takes its toll." Despite those wistful comments, most of us figured he would never step down and just continue on for eternity. And he probably would have, had God not planted the idea to step down in Peter's head thousands of years ago. Yes, it took a while to take hold, but God knew what He was doing, as

He knows all things. He was just preparing early, very early, and you know what He always tells us: **"Failure to Prepare is Preparing to Fail!"** You've probably also heard some of those very old sayings in the study of ancient religion. Things like, "All in God's time," or, "God is always on time." Well, this situation was a perfect example. God knew when His plan needed to be set in motion, and that time was here and now.

But how, exactly? How could all we Angels accomplish this great task in under twenty-four hours? We discussed it again and again. Several ideas were thrown out by various Angels. Some suggested only the remaining six Archangels in existence be eligible. Others wanted Michael to nominate a select few to narrow down the pool. Still others said we should vote to change the rules so we could just choose Raphael. Each time such ideas came up, Raphael reminded us of the three rules God had set forth.

Raphael put special emphasis on the eligibility rule and reminded us all to keep an open mind.

The Choirs of Angels had deliberated for hours unsuccessfully, which was very apparent by the diminishing glow from the halos of even the most-tenured Angels. We all needed a pep talk and Gabriel was there to provide it in our time of need. He summoned everyone's attention by sounding the supersonic golden trumpets, and then, having brought the Choirs to absolute silence, spoke as only an Archangel of his stature and wisdom could.

He said to us in a soft but stern voice, his long white beard moving in tune to the melody of his wisdom, "It's not about the old or new, or the easy or difficult choice. It's about us being given this task by God as a gift. It's about our nature as spiritual creatures who glorify God without ceasing and who serve His saving plans for other creatures. Simply put, it is about Loving and Giving and Serving!" After a round of thunderous applause had died down, he continued on, "If we focus on choosing an Angel that embodies these three ideals and follows them, no matter the circumstances on Heaven or Earth, then we will have made the right choice." To this, he received another roar of applause.

As the Angels cheered and applauded, a big, radiant smile shone down from God, whom I noticed watching us from far up in the clouds. His glory was unmistakable.

Once Gabriel's words sunk in, we all sprang into action, organizing into smaller Angel groups within the different levels of the Great Hall to focus our conversations. We compiled lists of potential candidates, who some suggested met the criteria, and looked long and hard, far and wide, to make sure no one was missed. In just a few hours we had narrowed our potentials from Infinity down to approximately one million Angels, which included some from each type of Angel. The lists ranged from over 500,000 Guardian Angels all the way down to just one hundred from my small group: the Angels in Training. Whatever the number, everyone included on the lists were thought to embody the tenets: Love, Give, and Serve. Not bad, considering where we started earlier in the process. We now had a workable list to narrow down further. We felt we were making great progress—until Raphael blared the trumpets and reminded us of our remaining time. Just under thirteen hours remained to make a final decision.

Things appeared bleak again. We universally decided that each group would once again break off on its own. This time, though, we were not nearly as excited as before, which could be seen in the slumping wings of many Angels. We looked for Gabriel as we broke off, hoping to hear some more words of encouragement from him to bolster our spirits. He was nowhere to be found, having been called off by God to help with an urgent matter. I remember thinking the timing was curious. It led some of us to grow even glummer, thinking we were being abandoned in our time of need. A sad thing indeed. Even as Angels we couldn't realize the importance of doing this the way God wanted. Luckily for us, not all Angels felt the same way. Inspired by the wisdom of God's grace, some remained confident God had a plan; we just had to figure out the best way to carry it out. We headed to our designated areas, located on various levels of the western block of stone meeting rooms, and got into our smaller groups. Thankfully, a few Angels with a lot more wisdom than I had at the time spoke up.

The Archangel Barachiel was helping lead our Angels in Training group, since we were a little lost with everything. Fortunately, Barachiel had a soft spot in his heart for us, which he always expressed with an ever-present look of both empathy and wisdom, conveyed upon his youthful face, framed by wavy gray hair. We reminded him of when he was still without wings, like us. Plus, Barachiel had been the youngest Archangel ever—until yours truly was elected. He had come to Heaven when he was only twenty-eight in Earth years and had received his regal-red Archangel robe and staff after only five hundred years in the hereafter.

You call me old, Anabeth. Think about that for a second. Consider a time, millions of millennia ago, when Barachiel had so much to figure out and learn in order to earn his wings, just like you do. Just remember, we've all been there, Anabeth. Most of us not only started out young like I did but also had the innocence of children. I see that smirk on your face, Anabeth. Yes, I was once innocent too!

It was a time when we all saw everything with wonder and awe as we attempted to understand the importance of it all. We tried to stay focused on doing our part. A lot of us found the notion that one of us might become an Archangel in a matter of hours laughable. Mostly we just focused on the task of ensuring we would have an answer when we were called upon. Some in our group thought we were participating in the selection process because God always involved everyone. Plus, it was the rules, so we had to be included.

Barachiel saw that our group was still struggling as we continued to argue and lose focus in our conversation. We needed encouragement, much like he often had back in the day, and the type of powerful wisdom only an Archangel could provide. He brought us to order with a resounding pound on the stone podium and shared three things. First, he told us we had to believe in ourselves. Next, that we had to have faith. And finally, that we could accomplish anything we put our minds to. Those were the most important lessons his mentor taught him, and now he was teaching them to us—much as I now teach you, Anabeth.

"Yes, you do, Teacher!"

Yes, Anabeth, I do. We knew Barachiel felt strongly about these beliefs, which he had lived by from his days as an Angel-in-Training to his current status as one of only seven Archangels at that time. His words were well-received by all the Angels in Training, but they especially resonated with one young Angel in the group: me.

I was part of the newest training group and had joined just a short century prior. This may seem like a long time to some, but it's minuscule in comparison to others. I was green—very green—and full of questions and wonder like you are today. I often interrupted my professors' lectures with a laundry list of questions that frequently took them off track. Sound familiar, Anabeth?

"Uh ... if you say so, Teacher."

I know I'm correct on that one, Anabeth.

Many thought my questioning nature funny. My professors considered it annoying, but a few of my peers actually found me inspiring and enjoyed my unique viewpoint. I looked at things through a different lens. Simply put, I was on a different level, my own level. Barachiel liked to compare me to some of the young prodigies in Earth history, like Mozart or Picasso. That always embarrassed me, by the way, which I think he secretly enjoyed.

"Kind of like the way you embarrass me sometimes!"

Yes, Anabeth, sometimes. In any case, much like those

prodigies, I wasn't taken seriously by a great many in Heaven. It could have been my young age or lack of experience, or perhaps they saw me as a threat. Most likely, though, I wasn't taken seriously because I just wasn't very serious.

Yes, Anabeth, I was a jokester. The type to play a prank whenever I had a chance. Most of these jokes were tied to my vanity, but some were just plain silly, like the time I hid old professor Moses's tablet. Professor Moses couldn't find it for a week. And when he did, let's just say he wasn't too happy about where he found it. That little prank earned me a month's worth of transcribing scrolls as punishment. I laughed it off when asked about it since I got to learn the Hebrew language during the transcription process. Crazy, right? That's what I was, a clown with a brain. An Angel-in-Training who considered myself smarter than all my professors. To be honest, I really didn't like showing my intelligence—except when playing an elaborate joke. I preferred to "fit in" and be just like everyone else. Though I wanted to keep things light-hearted and simple, Barachiel had other plans for me.

He told me I was destined for greatness and tried repeatedly to help me gain confidence in myself. That was an uphill battle. Barachiel, who saw a lot of himself in me—having been through similar trials and tribulations throughout his training—knew the only way I would achieve greatness was to believe—in myself, my faith, and my ability to do whatever I put my mind to. It thrilled Barachiel to think I was finally coming around, and at the most opportune time. He later told me he had finally seen the inspiration and motivation in my eyes that proved I was ready to fulfill my destiny. Still, Barachiel knew I needed prodding and spent some time trying to think of one big idea to get me going. One spark to light the fire that would propel me forward. Boy, was I stubborn. Sure, being allowed to help choose the newest Archangel was a big deal, it just wasn't *the* big deal Barachiel had in mind. He was thinking a little bigger and smaller at the same time.

Bigger in the sense that he knew who would be the perfect fit for the new Archangel and smaller in the sense that the perfect fit in his eyes happened to be little bitty me. A pretty hard sell—and for good reason, Anabeth. It was a stretch, to be sure. Most of the Angels in Training weren't exactly waiting to be picked for the opportunity. It had never happened before; we weren't even full Angels at that point—not yet bestowed with what most considered the most important part of being an Angel.

"Wings!"

That's right, Anabeth. Still, to his credit, Barachiel believed that I was ready, that I was able to Love, Give, and Serve everyone in Heaven and on Earth in the ways that were needed. He believed I could accomplish everything required for the position. And he knew, with all his heart, mind, and soul, that the next Archangel would be the jokester with all the questions. Now he just needed to convince me.

CHAPTER 3: THE SPARK

Barachiel tried to spark a fire—in a "Heaven" sort of way, of course—under my behind many times. Every time he thought he had a good plan, I would foil things at the last minute—and usually with the same silly antics I was known for. It was all so comical to me at the time, I chuckled just thinking about it.

"That's not very Angel-like!"

True, Anabeth. It wasn't, but I eventually learned my lesson. Each time he tried to reel me in, I would act as if I didn't know what was going on and laugh off his efforts. Barachiel knew the truth—that I was more cunning than him and always one if not three steps ahead. This failed to really frustrate Barachiel, as much as his annoyance may have seemed justified at the time. It just fueled his motivation, and he set his mind to coming up with new and better plans to rope me into the role. But this new situation was different. This time, Barachiel did not have the luxury to prepare a "plan of attack." He might have been discouraged, had it not been for the fire of certainty burning within him, as he later told me. This fire, in fact, helped him realize that time was indeed on his side. With only minutes left before the nominees were to be finalized, I would have zero time to dispute his decision. The urgency of the situation would require me to take whatever direction was given, with no questions asked, no time to think two steps ahead. Quite a disadvantage! It was exactly the type of situation that would force me into action, when Barachiel said I was at my best.

Full of excitement over the opportunity, yet realizing he could not form a full plan on his own this time, he sought God's help. Immediately, Barachiel dropped to his knees in the middle of our stone meeting room and prayed for God's grace.

"Right then and there?"

Yes, Anabeth, then and there. It wasn't super-unusual. You may think I pray a lot. Where do you think I learned it from?

"Ohhh!"

So, Barachiel prayed that the idea for a spark would find him, and he continued to do so for what he said felt like an eternity yet seemed to get no response. He realized he would have to seek out God Himself, and quickly. I remember him running out of our room as if his robe was on fire. He searched the north, south, east, and west bronze corridors and asked everyone lingering about the halls making their way to their designated rooms if they knew of God's current whereabouts. It wasn't until he saw Peter—easily recognizable with his unmistakable short brown goatee and flowing gold cloak worn only by the former Apostles—that he got excited. Peter was standing alone at the other end of the main cathedral corridor, waiting for the express observation tower elevator. Barachiel took off running like I had never seen before and made his way to Peter. I could faintly hear Him from where I was watching from the end of the west bronze corridor, as I had snuck out of the stone meeting room and followed him from a distance.

"Peter! Peter! Where is God?" Barachiel yelled as he approached.

Peter turned toward him, somewhat startled, and said, "God is still in a meeting with Gabriel and gave explicit orders that they not be disturbed."

Barachiel pressed, "But it's urgent. It's regarding the Archangel decision!"

Peter responded firmly, "You can *try* to interrupt Him, but He's 100,000 floors up in the oversight tower. Besides, you'll have to take the stairs. The elevator's *out of order!*"

I thought for sure that Barachiel would continue pressing Peter with his plight, but instead Barachiel enveloped him in a super-strong, angelic, heavenly embrace and kissed him on the cheek. "Thank you, Peter! You're a genius!" Barachiel yelled right into Peter's confused face. Then, smiling from ear to ear, Barachiel turned to head back down the cathedral corridor as I ran back to our Angel-in-Training room.

This was it! Barachiel had gotten the divine inspiration he needed, the spark to his brilliant idea—and it had come in the form of a broken elevator. No one, including me, understood his excitement. Barachiel said later he would have never guessed his spark would arrive in so unexpected a manner, and when he least expected it—yet exactly when he needed it. I knew something was going on when Barachiel returned excitedly, then paused for a moment to say, "Please, let me take a minute. I need to reflect on this opportunity to learn."

At the time I wondered what opportunity he was referring to, but I later realized this was typical of God. Always using the situation to teach one a lesson. Always letting us push and push, only to have something come so easily after we finally accepted His grace. Allowing us to struggle so little and yet feel like it is so much that we must be saved immediately. Giving us the opportunity to let His grace come at the perfect time. In short, Barachiel told me he thought it was God, Loving, Giving, and Serving Him the way He wanted done to all his children in Heaven and on Earth. Barachiel had received the answer directly from God. Tears still come to Barachiel's eyes when he shares this story, and to this day, Barachiel still thanks God for this wonderful gift and the future it would lead to. He thanked Him for helping in his time of need and promised that he would do better to be more aware of God's grace when it was given. Now, these are things we should all be praying for more often, wouldn't you agree, Anabeth?

"Yes, Teacher. You are correct."

I'd think you were mocking me if I didn't know better.

"Hehe!"

Very funny, Anabeth.

When Barachiel returned, we were not quite where he had left us. Sure, we were at the same stone meeting room where we always had our Angel In Training meetings, but the focus and determination of the group had somehow disappeared. Many Angels had become discouraged after already working on the problem for hours which was apparent by their less than radiant robes and faces. Instead of working on the matter of choosing an Archangel, some were sleeping, some were telling stories, and some were just not thinking. I was leading a small group of misfits in a different direction—the orchestration of a practical joke on Barachiel, which involved having us all vacate the room before his return, leaving him surprised and all alone. Yes, I know. Big surprise. I had wrongly assumed that Barachiel wouldn't be back for quite a while as he often took a long time walking through the corridors—he was frequently stopped by others requesting a discussion of some kind. Thus, Barachiel's expedient return took me by surprise. The look on my face when I saw him come through the wood and copper-framed door must have been priceless. It was the look of someone who knew they had messed up and were in big trouble.

Barachiel advanced to the front of the group to speak to us. I thought for sure he was about to scold me in public and teach me a lesson on humility, so I casually gave him half my attention.

"That's not very Angel-like!" Anabeth commented for the second time during my story.

Yes, Anabeth, you're again correct. It wasn't. You can bet I straightened up when I heard Barachiel say, "The group will have to continue without Ezra for now. He has been called to meet with God."

A verbal "OMG" collectively emerged from our group; we simply could not believe our ears. Called to meet with God? Whatever for? Most thought this meant I had definitely crossed the line. That I would finally be punished for all my sins. My thought? That I was in *seriously* big trouble! Some of my peers laughed, some patted me on the back and offered condolences, and a few actually said their last goodbyes as I walked off with Barachiel.

"Ohhh, I bet you were about to get it!"

Sorry, Anabeth. This time you're incorrect.

The Big Idea

I didn't *get it,* as you assumed, Anabeth. Barachiel walked me out to the lower south garden and sat me down on one of the beautiful hand-made gold benches that adorned the lush greenery. Even with my impending consequences looming ahead, I didn't have time for fear. I was too busy assessing the situation, as I frequently did in times of stress. I tried to read Barachiel's body language and overall demeanor. Unfortunately, he wasn't giving me much. He just sat there quietly with his eyes closed and hands folded, clearly praying, as he often did prior to teaching. When Barachiel finally opened his eyes, he looked at me with deep compassion, then placed his arm on my shoulder and said softly, "God needs your help and wants you to go down to Earth. He will meet you there."

A *WTH?* look came across my face as a multitude of questions came to mind. *Help with what? Why? When? How? Where?* I was trying to figure out which question to ask first when Barachiel stood up and motioned for me to do the same. "Okay, time to go!" he announced, and with that, he simply took my hand and led me to the Earth Express Elevator.

23

The Earth Express Elevator—or EEE, as we called it—was the only way Angels could descend to Earth way back then. We didn't have all the luxuries that you enjoy today, Anabeth.

"I remember reading something about the EEE in an old book I found in the training library!"

Well … since your old book didn't seem to say much, let me tell you about the EEE. It was mainly used by the Guardian Angels since they traveled to Earth and back the most frequently. The EEE was both a marvel and mystery. It was not round or square, oval or triangular. In fact, it did not have a true shape to it at all—except for the shape of imagination. Completely translucent—though not made of glass or any such substance—like the little fish that glow deep in the sea. There were no real sides, roof, or even a floor, which made it seem as if it were skintight around the rider yet projected on forever. It moved faster than the speed of light without the whir of an engine or hum of a turbine. It was utterly silent and truly remarkable, even by Heaven's standards. The most impressive thing was that it could take you anywhere on Earth in the blink of an eye. And now, I was about to board it for the first time.

I did my best to stay still despite being visibly frightened. I waited patiently with Barachiel on the one-hundred-mile-high suspended landing platform but didn't say a word; I was once again too busy thinking. I was about to meet with God face-to-face for the first time and help Him in some way. I couldn't believe this was happening. I had been directly in front of God only once, when I first arrived in Heaven, but it was a very brief encounter as I came from Earth and passed through the Pearly Gates.

Before you interrupt me, Anabeth, yes, I know God is with us always, as He is with all of His children in Heaven and on Earth. But this was different because it was tough for me to feel God's presence all the time.

"What!? You weren't able to feel God's presence all the time?"

Yes, Anabeth, you're right—in part.

You see, Heaven and Earth were a little different than they are today. Back then, both Angels and humans could only feel God's presence when they opened themselves to let it in. Sure, His presence was always there; it just wasn't constantly flowing through us, as it does for you and me now. Today, God's presence is whatever we need in the moment. For most of us, it feels like pure Love. For those on Earth, it can feel like a warm blanket on a cold winter night or a cool breeze on a hot summer day, all at the same time. It's difficult to explain by today's standards, but it felt like pure Love and was very special if you allowed it in. I loved the sensation—when I chose to embrace it. Those times when I closed it off were the most difficult, when I ended up feeling very sad and alone. Come to think of it, I usually closed it off when I was up to no good, like pranking my professors.

"Not too bright."

Yes, Anabeth, true enough. I was a fool at times, quite a fool.

"You can leave that lesson out. I don't need to know how to be a fool!"

25

Don't worry, Anabeth. You're already learning more than I ever did.

And so, as I stood there waiting for the EEE, I tried to take comfort in knowing that God truly was with me always and would be in our meeting for sure. I prayed and talked with God each day. This would surely be no different, I remember telling myself. Only my mind also kept telling me it would be different. I was about to stare straight into the eyes of The Lord God Almighty, The Heavenly Father, The Creator, The Most-High. The One who knew more about me than I knew about myself and, more importantly, knew all my sins. Still, I tried to act calm and mature in front of Barachiel. I composed myself as the EEE arrived, then thanked Barachiel and gave him a warm embrace. Barachiel smiled and waved goodbye as I boarded the elevator.

The very old elevator attendant with the hunched back and flowing yellow robe that seemed to go on forever, Cain, welcomed me inside and closed the door.

"You said the EEE didn't have a door!"

Correct as usual, Anabeth. I couldn't actually see the door, but I couldn't see Barachiel anymore either, so I figured some type of barrier or partition had to be involved.

Cain could tell I was nervous and watched me with a wry old smile. "Don't worry, kid," he said. "You'll be fine. Just close your eyes and it will all be over before you know it."

"Huh?" I murmured and closed my eyes as instructed. Before Cain could reply, I felt like I wasn't in Heaven anymore. At first, it was a feeling—or, shall we say, a lack thereof.

I tried to feel God's presence. Nothing. I had left it behind when the elevator started its motion. Something felt different now. I opened my eyes to a wondrous sight. Where was I? Not only wasn't I in Heaven any longer, but Cain was now gone too. More importantly, I was no longer in the EEE ... or was I? Sure, I was still in an elevator, but now it seemed different, quite unlike the other elevators in Heaven. It now looked old and worn, like the ones I remembered back from my time on Earth.

"Boy, that must have been really old."

It was indeed, Anabeth. This elevator was quite large and had a boxy shape. Dark faux wood walls on each side, with mirrors running across the top, and a ceiling with about a hundred tiny glowing light bulbs on it that kind of looked like the stars if you squinted and imagined really hard. A soft, red-carpeted floor lay beneath my feet, and the double stainless-steel doors projected a slightly distorted reflection of yourself if you gazed at them. It was then that I noticed I had taken human form, like the Guardian Angels often did on Earth. I no longer wore my Angel-in-Training light blue robe, clothed instead in a pressed, collared white shirt, brown khaki pants, and brown shoes. My glowing halo was gone, replaced by my original Earthly, short, brown hair, with no trace of the radiance of Heaven to be seen. Unfortunately, my human form wasn't any taller or grander than it had been during my mortal days, as I noticed I stood only at about five feet, eight inches. A panel off to the right on one of the walls caught my eye. White buttons numbered one through forty covered the panel in neatly aligned rows, along with a small LED pad with an arrow pointing down and blinking. This obviously wasn't the EEE, so what kind of elevator was it? Where was I? And more importantly, where was God?

I tried to focus. Did I miss some instructions from Barachiel? Was I supposed meet God on a certain floor? I felt myself getting flustered, so I took a deep breath, closed my eyes, and began to pray. I prayed that I would know what to do, that I would soon figure it all out and feel God's presence once again. Most of all, I prayed that God would soon be with me to give me all the answers. Just as I was getting deep into prayer, I heard a ding and opened my eyes.

"And what did you see?"

The elevator doors opened. Ten people—as in Earth people, you know, actual human beings—boarded the elevator. Crowded around me were men and women of various ages dressed in traditional Earthly attire, for the most part. Some carried briefcases or purses, a few were on their cell phones, and a couple were in mid-conversation. None of them seemed to notice me, which made me wonder, *Can they see me? Am I still invisible to them?* I hardly had a second to ponder this when a petite young teenage girl standing near the door, whose clothing and looks seemed disjointed, looked straight at me and said, "Hey, buddy! What floor do you need?"

I tried to think of an appropriate response but could only murmur, "Down, I'm-I'm going down. Thank you."

The young girl shrugged her shoulders and pushed the Door Close button.

The elevator began to descend. It started to pick up speed, and the lights blinked as it passed the different floors. Just as it seemed to reach full speed a loud noise emerged all around us, as if metal were grinding against metal, which caused the elevator to come to an abrupt, screeching halt. Everyone let out a collective gasp; a few people actually screamed. We all looked at each other in disbelief and then studied our surroundings, quickly trying to assess the situation. The elevator had come to a complete stop and seemed stable. Once we settled, we realized the floor indicator now read 12.

We were all very surprised and slightly frozen. A man in the corner whose face and clothing were equally weathered, with an accompanying smell that wasn't particularly surprising, said half-jokingly, "Well, folks. It looks like we're on the twelfth floor. Whose stop is this?"

A couple of people chuckled softly but soon realized no one else was laughing. Those laughing quickly stopped when a tall, slender lady toward the back said with the authority of a high school principal, "It seems we are stuck. Young lady, can you please press the Door Open button?" She motioned to the young teenage girl by the door.

The young girl pushed the indicated button over and over as if her repeated pressing might have an impact, but the doors remained shut. She tried a few other buttons, to no effect. A very large man whose size dwarfed the petite girl nudged her aside with the bump of a lineman and said in a southern accent, "Let me try, little missy." His thumb jammed into all the same buttons—including the Fire and Call buttons—as if his massive fleshy fingers would have more impact than hers, with zero success. A young, boy-next-door-looking man standing behind him winked at the young girl and quietly made a funny face with his tongue out toward the back of the large southern man. The girl laughed loudly, as if amongst a group of schoolgirls, then quickly contained herself when the large southern man gave her the stink eye as if he somehow knew she was laughing at him.

"Was his stink eye like the look you give me when I'm doing something I shouldn't be?"

Yes, Anabeth. It was.

The young girl looked back at "boy next door" with a smile of approval. He acknowledged her smile with one of his own while holding up his phone and said, "Sorry. No cell phone coverage in here."

A very anxious-looking man with shoulders that slumped forward from an apparent lifetime of insecurity blurted out in a frightened tone, "This is *not* funny, you guys!" He continued with even greater concern, "We are stuck and can't contact anyone from inside this metal box."

The tall slender lady spoke up once again in her principal's voice. "I'm sure building security will be along in a few minutes. We just need to be patient and remain calm."

A pretty young mother with glamour-shot hair and accompanying makeup, who was carrying a tiny infant in a body sling so that its slightly restless form rested against her belly, softly chimed in. "That's easy for you to say. My baby should be waking up hungry any minute now."

A frail old woman with platinum-gray hair and small glasses hanging from a chain chimed in. "You'll be okay, dear. I have seven kids and twenty-two grandchildren. I'll help you if you need anything. Besides, babies are resilient."

The confidence in the frail old woman's voice visibly soothed the young mother, who smiled back as she whispered, "Thank you."

Standing close to her husband, a quiet, conservative-looking woman lowered her head sadly as she overheard the conversation. Her seemingly very loving husband noticed and put his arm around her, pulling her closer and hugging her tightly in definitive consolation.

I stood there, taking all of this in but not saying a word. I was too busy wondering what was going on. My internal barrage of questions began again. *Who are all these people? What am I doing with them? Where did they come from? When will the elevator be fixed? Why isn't God here to take care of everything?* My head was spinning. I couldn't answer any of these questions and had no idea what to do.

"You mean you *didn't have all the answers?"*

Yes, Anabeth. That's correct. Situations were typically not all that difficult for me, but this one was disconcertingly different. I couldn't figure any of it out. Everything was so foreign and strange. I felt like a fish out of water bouncing around on the sand, gasping for air. So, I did the only thing I could think of. I closed my eyes and once again prayed.

No sooner had my eyes closed when the frail old woman tugged on my arm. "You okay, sonny?" she asked. "You look a little pale." She pulled a small water bottle out of her large purse and said, "Here, drink some water. You'll feel better."

I grabbed the bottle and took a small sip. "Thank you, Ma'am. You were right," I told her, then proceeded to chug the rest of the bottle until I realized everyone in the elevator was staring at me. Moderately embarrassed, I quickly ceased my guzzling and closed the bottle. "I'm fine, everyone." I offered a smile. "My name is Ezra. It's very nice to meet you all. What are your names?"

CHAPTER 4: THE INTRODUCTIONS

"*You said that!? And you told them your real name?*"

Yes, Anabeth. Of course I did! Angels always tell the truth. Besides, I still didn't know exactly where I was, and I wanted to learn more about them. My question seemed to come as a bit of a surprise to many in the elevator, just as it did to you, Anabeth. We were all pondering how to get out of our predicament when my question instantly changed the dynamic among us, turning it from moderately tense to relaxed. Which was good, since I had wanted to lighten the mood. After all, I was used to the temperaments of Heaven's Angels, which were usually pretty serene, as one would imagine. The tension in the elevator made me recall faint memories of my time on Earth long ago, which made me feel uncomfortable. Plus, I wanted to learn more about my fellow elevator-mates, as I frequently did with all I came across. My actions also set the stage for what would become a very interesting time for all of us. For the next hour or so, everyone in the elevator took turns introducing themselves and telling their personal stories. This occurred centuries ago, as you know, but I still remember it all so vividly, like it was yesterday.

Betty

The frail old woman with small glasses hanging from a chain was the first to jump in. "Hi, everyone! My God-given name is Beth-Anne, but nobody knows that 'cause it's not even on my driver's license. And yes, I can still drive, in case you're wondering! I've gone by Betty for as long as I can remember, and that's a mighty long time, considering I just celebrated my eightieth birthday last week!"

Everyone replied with various forms of "Happy Birthday" to Betty for the next minute, which seemed to send Betty off on a bit of a tangent. "It was so wonderful! My children threw me a beautiful surprise party. I didn't even have a clue that it was happening. There was catered food and drinks and cake, lots of chocolate cake. That's my favorite flavor, by the way. It was at the hall where I play bingo, and all my friends were there. We even had live music, balloons, streamers, and decorations in my favorite color, pink. I love that color. I have a lot of pink stuff in my home, as any old lady rightly should!"

This brought laughs and smiles from a few in the elevator.

She continued on to share how all seven of her children attended her party, along with all twenty-two of her grandchildren. The youngest six grandchildren even did a little dance performance at the party that she especially appreciated. Betty shared that it was very special because she didn't get to see her children and grandchildren as much as she used to, mostly due to the distance involved. The drive to many of them was too far for her to go on her own. She missed them all so dearly and longed to hug their sweet faces. Just as Betty was sharing the last part, she realized she had begun to shed a couple tears. Hastily, she reached into a large bag—which must have been a purse, although it had about three or four other bags stuffed inside it—and began digging around.

The large southern man said, "Here you go, Ma'am," as he offered her his handkerchief, then continued with, "Always good to have an extra hankie on hand for a woman's tears."

Betty waved him off, nudging his hand away and saying in a suddenly abrasive tone that caught me and the others by surprise, "Thank you, but I'm fine! It's just my allergies. They always act up this time of year."

The man slowly retreated his offering with a slight look of rejection and then gazed around. "Howdy, y'all. I'm Big John!"

John

Big John was called that for a reason. He stood about six feet, four inches and must have weighed over 250 pounds in Earth weight. He was definitely southern in more ways than his accent. Long days on the ranch had tanned his face, which was accented with a finely groomed mustache that turned down at the ends. He wore a silver-buttoned navy sport coat paired blue jeans, below which were brown cowboy boots fashioned from some kind of strange leather that looked rare and costly and were capped in silver tips that I assumed could be used in horseback riding. His silver belt buckle was about the size of Texas, where he coincidentally said he was from. The only thing missing to complete the ensemble was a cowboy hat, which he held in his right hand; a metal briefcase was clutched in his left. Big John continued on to share that he was in the building to take care of some business with his oil companies. He had learned the oil business straight out of high school while working with his daddy. Over the last twenty-five years, he had learned as much as he could working in different areas of oil. He started his own business about fifteen years ago, which had grown to be worth about $100 million at present. You could tell he was very proud of it. "My daddy always said, 'You can't put a price on the value of a hard day's work.' Well, I've put in a lot of hard days, and it's gotten me a company worth a whole lotta money! Guess daddy was wrong!" His southern chuckle echoed off the close-set walls before he continued. "And another thing! People are always saying you can't buy time. Well, my time is pretty valuable, and I know I'm losing a lot of money being stuck in this here elevator."

For a second that reminded us all of the predicament we were in until the tall woman spoke up. "I'm sure we won't be here very much longer. Oh, and I'm Olivia. Nice to meet everyone."

Olivia

Olivia could be described in Earth's terms as a very professional woman.

"Like a high school principal?"

Yes, Anabeth. That's how I described her based on a faint memory I had of my time on Earth. She wore a striped blue pantsuit and clear-rimmed glasses. She was holding a very fancy leather attaché case in her left hand, which caught my attention, leading me to notice the well-worn indentation on her ring finger—despite the lack of a wedding ring. Tall and slender with black hair put up tightly in a bun. Not a wrinkle on her suit nor a hair out of place, which seemed to symbolize how she carried herself.

"Your description sounds just like what I've seen in pictures."

Yes, Anabeth. I know you love those old books. Olivia was strong in appearance but brief in her introduction. I could tell she wanted to keep things superficial, even though she shared a lot more than she realized. Oliva had been a corporate attorney for almost thirty years, although her latest company, where she had a meeting that day, had employed her for just six months.

It seemed as if that was all she was going to share until Betty interrupted. "My son is in corporate law. Do you like it?"

Olivia answered Betty reluctantly, but something seemed to trigger her to open up. "I started my career in the district attorney's office when I was fresh out of law school. That's essentially why I decided to go to law school in the first place. My mom was a district attorney for over thirty-five years, and she was my role model." She realized we were waiting for more details and added, "After a year in the DA's office, I realized I wasn't getting the fulfillment that my mom always raved about, so I moved over to corporate law. I specialize in mergers and acquisitions now, which offers a lot more fringe benefits. That's *my* fulfillment!" Abruptly, she realized she was uncomfortably pointing at herself, so she found the easiest person to deflect our attention to. Once again, she motioned to the young teenage girl. "That's enough about me. Why don't you introduce yourself next, young lady?"

Faith

The young petite teenage girl looked up at Olivia sheepishly. I could tell she was not just uncomfortable but shy as well. "Uh, okay. I can go if you want. I'm Faith," she murmured. "This is my first time stuck in an elevator, so I'm new to this. I don't really know what to say."

Boy-next-door then piped in with, "Just tell us the usual stuff. You know, all the things your grandma would want to know if she called you out of the blue on a Tuesday afternoon." He looked over at Betty as he was finishing his sentence, who clearly took a little offense at his comments.

Faith noticed and said, "I get what you mean now. Well, let's see. I'm sixteen, and I go to St. Joseph's High School. No, wait. I used to go to St. Joseph's. I just transferred to Roosevelt."

Betty jumped in to interrupt just like she had before. "That's too bad, honey. I went to St. Joseph's way back when it was an all-girls school. As a matter of fact, all my kids went there too. It's an excellent school."

Boy-next-door, clearly worried that Betty might ramble on again, hastily kept the conversation going. "Sixteen? Are you driving yet, Faith?" he asked.

"No, I don't have my license yet, since I'm kind of afraid to drive. Besides, my parents don't really have time to teach me, since they split up."

I remember feeling sad for her. The same thing had happened to me when I was on Earth. I started to pray for her and then Betty once again chimed in. "How about sports? They always have excellent teams at St. Joseph's."

Faith obliged Betty with an answer. "I don't play any sports now, although I played soccer for a long time. Just not in high school. I lost interest in it after ... uh ... I mean it just became not as fun as it used to be." Faith's voice had cracked a bit during that last statement, and you could tell she was beginning to get more uncomfortable sharing and having all of our eyes on her. Much like Olivia had looked when she passed the baton to Faith.

Faith was about to be bailed out by boy-next-door again, when a very soft and mildly high-pitched voice said, "I guess I'll get this over with." I turned to face the owner of that voice: the very anxious man with the slumped shoulders who had been scared earlier when we first got stuck.

"Oh, yeah. I thought that part was funny."

Now, that's not very Angel-like, Anabeth.

"Sorry, Teacher. Please continue."

Percy

The man looked up, seeming even more frightened than he had been when our elevator first got stuck.

"Ha, Ha."

Okay, Anabeth, okay. Still, he managed to give us his name in a soft tone: Percy.

Big John automatically stuck out his hand. "Good to meet you, Percy."

Percy reluctantly shook John's hand, even as it seemed to envelop his small one completely.

"What kind of work do you do here?" John inquired.

Percy answered with the same hesitance that he had begun his introduction with. He told us that he was an accountant in the building for a small, family-owned company. He had worked for the last fifteen years, ever since he finished college. He said he got into accounting because he liked the safety and security of it. He was about to continue about his job when surprisingly Olivia spoke up:

"I can always use good accountants in mergers and acquisitions," she announced.

Percy responded with, "Thank you, Ma'am, but I'm good where I am, doing basic bookkeeping. I don't know about that stuff, anyways. There's no ambiguity with bookkeeping, and no one can complain if you're wrong. It's just all about the numbers being incorrect and not me."

Olivia turned up her nose a bit and murmured, "I'm sorry I asked," under her breath.

"Human beings can be so mean!"

Yes, Anabeth, they can be at times. I knew Percy heard her, but he was too timid to respond. He just kind of paused and smiled nervously at us all. Things grew tense for a few seconds until a small squeal and coo came from the little baby. This really caught the attention of the young couple. The man not only tightened his arm around his wife but reached over with his other arm to hold her hand. I literally could feel their love from where I was standing. The couple's sudden change in body language made them the center of attention, which Percy was happy to relinquish. We all turned our eyes toward them, ready to learn more.

Eva and Adam

It was clear to me and everyone else that the man knew he was in a crowded elevator with a bunch of strangers but didn't seem to care about how his obvious public display of affection might be taken. He loosened his loving grasp on his wife slightly and said, "Sorry, this is my wife Eva, and I'm Adam and ... as I'm sure you can tell, I really, really love her!"

Everyone including me laughed at Adam's comment and willingness to make fun of himself. He proceeded to tell us all a little about them while mixing some quasi-humor into each sentence. "I know we look like we're newlyweds, but we've actually been married for over eleven years. We met in grad school and have been pretty much inseparable ever since." He gave her a half-hug. Eva smiled widely and looked at Adam with love and admiration each time he spoke but remained silent, so Adam continued. "I don't work in the building. I'm just in boring computer programming. Now, Eva here, she's the one with the fun job. Eva is the best social worker in town, and she has the patience of a saint. I mean, she has to in her line of work."

I remember chuckling to myself at his saint comment.

"I would have chuckled too!"

She did seem very sweet, Anabeth.

"What do you do, honey?" Betty asked Eva directly.

Eva responded with her own degree of unassuming confidence. "I work, um, I mean, I have the pleasure of working with special needs children every day."

She continued a bit more, telling us how wonderful and rewarding the work was. It was interesting to note that about half of the folks in the elevator gave her warm smiles and nods of approval, while the other half seemed disinterested. I had an idea why but kept it to myself. None seemed more disinterested than Betty, who had asked the question in the first place. This helped to tell me her true opinion on the matter.

Betty showed her disapproval of what Eva was saying by cutting her off and asking yet another question. "What about children of your own, dear? You must have some cute little rug rats, like my grandbabies."

Eva's demeanor quickly changed; she was about to respond when Adam did for her. "Not yet, but we hope to be blessed with some real soon."

I, along with everyone else, could feel things growing uncomfortable again, when just as coincidentally as the baby had interrupted before, she did so again—although not with a squeal or a cry. Infusing some instant levity into our situation, as only a baby could, she let out a very loud fart.

"Babies are so cute!"

Yes, Anabeth. She was. Cute or not, it was hard to believe that big noise—along with the corresponding smell—could come out of that tiny baby. We all laughed quite loudly at the little baby gas bomb and her perfect timing when the pretty young mother said, "I'm so sorry. I better check her diaper."

This brought a natural pause to our conversation. A few people busied themselves checking their phones, only to realize they still did not have coverage. Others just shifted their balance and looked around, all while I tried to just soak it all in. Boy-next-door, who had tried to rescue Faith before Percy, chimed in and said, "Well, we've heard from a lot of you already, so I'll go next."

Joshua

I remember thinking that this young man seemed apprehensive about the situation yet comfortable at the same time. The best way I could describe it was that he talked like someone who had learned to speak in front of large groups by envisioning the audience in their underwear.

"Huh?"

I know it sounds funny, Anabeth, but I learned that down on Earth. It means he had an aura of confidence about him that didn't come easily, more forced than natural.

"I get it now."

Good, Anabeth.

He stood a little taller as he announced, "My name is Joshua." Joshua told us that he worked in the building in finances. He wasn't married and didn't even have a girlfriend. At the time I thought that a bit odd, as he was a good-looking young man by typical Earth standards. He was not quite as tall as Big John but close, and definitely in better physical condition. Someone—I think the woman with the baby—asked him if he was an athlete. He replied that he had been a swimmer in college and still really enjoyed working out. I think she was trying to flirt with him, but he remained very polite, at a slight emotional distance. He told us that he didn't really have time for a girlfriend, since he volunteered a lot at Big Brother.

"What's Big Brother?"

Big Brother is an organization on Earth where men mentor young boys who don't have fathers or positive role models. Definitely one of the better programs they had at that time. Kind of like the Angel mentorship programs you belong to, Anabeth.

"Oh, cool!"

Overall, Joshua seemed a very well-mannered and put-together young man, but I still knew something was a bit off when he said, "I don't deserve to talk this much about myself. I want to know more about you." He moved his finger around the elevator until he found someone who hadn't introduced themself yet. I thought he was about to point to me, but his finger paused on the form of the weathered and disheveled man.

Matt

It was funny the way things progressed from there. The man he pointed at looked so surprised, his expression resembling mine whenever I would play a prank on Moses and then get caught and have to face the consequences. I hated that feeling, and this man seemed to not like being called out either. In any case, he responded to the tip of Joshua's pointed finger with: "You can call me Matt, although I'm not much for introductions. I really just wanna get out of here and have a smoke. I'm just an old vet, that's all."

Before you ask, Anabeth, vet is short for veteran—someone who served in Earth's military during one of their many horrible wars.

"I get it."

Good, Anabeth. Matt told us he was in the building to see his doctor, which he hated doing and so hadn't scheduled an appointment in years, but something had come up that required him to go more frequently. At the time I remember being tempted to apply some of my Angelic abilities to figure out Matt's health issues, but I knew it wouldn't have been right. So, I refrained.

"I was thinking I would have done the same thing."

Yes, I know you were, Anabeth, which is why I shared my decision with you. Wink, wink. Matt said he wasn't married and didn't have family anymore. He now lived alone in a trailer outside of town. I felt strong empathy for him, hearing the loneliness and sadness in his words, but I kept it to myself, not wanting to reveal my true identity. Matt was another person in our group who wasn't really comfortable speaking. Just as Joshua had, he looked around, then stopped when he saw that the baby was now unwrapped from her blanket and awake. I noticed a single tear glistening in the corner of Matt's eye, but he didn't draw attention to it. Instead, he just paused and then said, "She reminds me of my daughter. What's her name?"

Carly

The pretty young mother responded, "This is Jo, short for Josephine. We named her after my grandmother, who passed right before she was born. So, she's like an Angel."

"Like an Angel?"

People on Earth often refer to their babies as Angels, Anabeth.

"That's funny!"

Yes, Anabeth, I suppose it is, to us. The pretty young mother introduced herself as Carly. Looking closely, I noticed she was not pretty in the natural sense of the word. Her beauty was forced, as if she were trying to build a façade, a false appearance, to show the world. She had blond hair that appeared colored on a regular basis and perfect makeup as if hours had been spent applying it that morning. Both she and Jo were dressed in designer-label clothing from head to toe. Jo was only three months old, Carly informed us, and was scheduled for a checkup with a pediatrician in the building that day. Everything had always checked out perfectly with Jo, except for her eating. She wasn't getting enough breast milk, so Carly was going to have to supplement with baby formula. Betty told her that she could probably get her some, as her daughter was a rep for a formula company. Carly really appreciated that fact, since she didn't really care for breastfeeding anyway. She still felt very new to motherhood and learning it all. I could tell that it was very challenging for her, and her reluctance with everything seemed to indicate that she wasn't enjoying motherhood as most young mothers on Earth would with a beautiful little gift from God like Jo.

I felt empathy for her as I listened but knew I was the only one left in the elevator to take over the conversation. So, I finally spoke up. I was about to impart some Angelic wisdom about babies being a blessing when I remembered I wasn't with my peers but a group of humans who didn't know who and what I was. I realized I should probably share something a bit more basic.

"Definitely a better idea."

Yes, Anabeth. I thought so too.

Me

"Hello Everyone! My name is Ezra, as I said earlier. I don't work in the building and am not from around here."

"Where are you from?" Big John and Betty asked me simultaneously.

"I'm just passing through, really. I've never been in the building and am only here today to meet a friend. Well, actually, I haven't reached my friend yet because we all got stuck first."

"Where does your friend work?" inquired Joshua. "Maybe I know him."

"He doesn't work in the building either," I quickly added. "We were just supposed to meet here. Plus, I'm not sure I have all the details right, so I was still trying to track him down when I came across all of you nice people."

"That's kind of you to say, young man. Tell us more about yourself," urged Betty.

I froze for a few seconds, trying to think of a response.

"That would be scary."

Yes, Anabeth. It really was. I had to tell the truth but couldn't tell them who I was, so I just listed off some things that they had shared too.

"I am not working yet, as I'm trying to finish up school to become a teacher" was the first thing I blurted out.

"Where do you go to school?" Faith asked me.

I pretended not to hear her and continued as quickly as I could. "Let's see. I'm not married, and I don't have any children or pets, and … that about sums it up. Gee, how much longer do you think we will be stuck in here?" Thank God my distracting question worked, or at least I thought it did.

Eyes Wide Open

Everyone was starting to get restless when Olivia once again said, "It's been well over an hour. Security has to arrive soon."

Big John quickly responded. "Wait a gosh-darn minute! It's after 8 p.m. Franklin from security always locks up the building and leaves exactly at 8 p.m. to pick up his wife. I know, 'cause I'm usually the last one out of the building right there with him. Sorry to say this, y'all, but I don't think anyone knows we're here."

"No!" exclaimed Percy. "You mean we're stuck here all night? I can't … I can't … I can't be here all night. Who's going to feed my cat? I need to get out of here!" He was hyperventilating and clearly struggling to stay in control.

Unfortunately, he wasn't the only one. Right then, little baby Jo started crying, as if Percy's loud complaints had pinched her baby skin and woken her from a deep sleep. Carly was tearing up right along with her baby as she tried to console her. Betty started digging through her bag frantically and talking gibberish. Joshua and Olivia both kept trying to call out on their cell phones. Faith selected random buttons on the elevator to repeatedly press. Matt started pacing back and forth in the corner, and Eva and Adam hugged each other tightly. All this unfolded within just a matter of seconds.

I felt very bad and responsible. After all, it was my question that had started the panic in the first place. I closed my eyes to pray for what I had done. I struggled immediately. The wave of human emotions kept washing over me, making it impossible to concentrate. It was unlike anything I had felt at the time and like nothing I can compare it to so you can understand or relate, Anabeth. It was stronger and more powerful than I could handle for long. Desperately, I closed my eyes tighter and tried to pray even harder. I asked God to take it all away. I asked him to help me, to come and save me from everything! But nothing happened.

"Nothing?!"

Yes, Anabeth, nothing. At least nothing in the sense that you're used to in Heaven. When you ask for God's help in Heaven, what happens, Anabeth?

"I instantly receive help from God."

Exactly, Anabeth. That's how it is now in Heaven. But I was not in Heaven; I was stuck in the elevator on Earth—and on Earth, God allows humans to make choices and exert free will. So in fact, He is present on Earth, but not the same way as in Heaven. On Earth, one must have faith and trust that God is with you at all times.

"Ohh, I understand now! So, when did you understand?"

Not as quickly as you did, Anabeth. I needed more help, which I received in a different way.

As I said, I had closed my eyes to pray and ask God to help me. When I didn't get the kind of response I had grown accustomed to, I figured I had to try something different. So, I left my eyes open wide, absorbing as much as I could from my surroundings and everyone in the room. I prayed not only with open eyes but with an open heart and mind. I started to recite scripture, such as **Matthew 21:22: "If you believe, you will receive whatever you ask for in prayer."** I told myself over and over that I was there to Love, Give, and Serve my new friends in the elevator. I prayed for God to give me the strength to help everyone else and no longer prayed for myself.

"What happened?"

God answered my prayers, Anabeth. Suddenly, I was able to handle the wave of emotions, to focus and come to peace. And suddenly, I knew I was indeed there to help everyone inside of that elevator—not just in that moment but for a lifetime. Suddenly, I knew what I had to do.

I took the strength God was providing and put it to work immediately. "Everyone! Everyone! Can you all settle down for a minute, please? I have an idea. "

They quieted down and listened.

"I've been standing here praying to myself and realized I was leaving you all out of those prayers, which is completely unfair. First, please forgive me for that. Second, the Bible says in **Matthew 18:20: 'For where there are two or three gathered together in my name, there I am in the midst of them.'** I can really use your help with this. Will you all take a moment to pray with me?"

They all just stared at me like I'd lost my mind. I kept my eyes opened wide and gave them the biggest calming smile of acceptance I possibly could. I extended my arms and reached out my hands to take the pair closest to me.

I stood there that way, hands still out, waiting for what felt like an eternity, so I said, "It will be okay. Take my hands."

Carly took my left hand, and Matt my right. Percy then took Carly's hand, and Eva took Matt's. She was already holding Adam's hand, who reached toward Joshua. Joshua accepted and then grasped Betty's. I couldn't believe this was actually working—until Betty reached for Big John's hand, and he simply stared down at it without extending his own.

"I'm not really much for prayer. Y'all go ahead," he said as he crossed his arms.

Upon hearing his comment Olivia said something I

couldn't hear under her breath and then grabbed Faith's hand. Faith reached out for Matt's hand, which would have closed the circle without Big John. In a moment of pure emotion, I yelled, "Please stop!"

Everyone suddenly let go, gawking at me in surprise. I re-extended my hands and said with the authority of a Sunday school teacher, "We are all going to participate, including you, Big John. We are all in this elevator together, and therefore we *all* need to pray together!"

He gave me an annoyed look.

I spoke again before he could respond. "Don't worry, Big John. You don't have to say a word. I'll do all the talking."

"Okay, then, sonny. Just this once," he replied with clear reluctance.

Everyone once again clasped hands and looked at me expectantly.

"First off, thank you all for participating and allowing me the opportunity to pray with you. It is truly an honor and pleasure to be here with everyone, despite our situation. Although I usually close my eyes and bow my head to pray, I think I'll leave my eyes open so I can see you all as I pray for you."

And so I began ...

"Heavenly Father,

We thank you for bringing us all together tonight. We thank you for the wonderful opportunity to meet new friends, to learn more about them, and to share in this experience with one another. We know that this may come with its own challenges, and we accept these as gifts from you. We acknowledge that our time together is truly a blessing and worthy of your presence, and we pray that it will be filled with your love and grace. We make ourselves 100 percent available to the gift of your grace, as we know that it was given to us through the sacrifice of your Son and our Lord and Savior Jesus Christ. We ask that the Holy Spirit watch over us and help guide us in our thoughts and actions. We pray that everything we do will be in accordance with your will, and we pray that our eyes will be wide open to all your amazing possibilities. Amen."

As I prayed, I made sure I looked deeply into the eyes of each person in the elevator. I wanted them to know that my prayers were for them and about them, but I also wanted to look deeper. I drew on my Angelic abilities as I prayed and looked into their hearts and souls.

"Really? What did you see?"

Quite a bit, Anabeth.

I saw what was driving the wave of emotions I had felt earlier, all of their struggles, fears, insecurities, weaknesses, and pain. I saw the reasons why each of them needed my help. I saw that they needed to be shown better paths than the ones they were on. In short, I saw how I would not only Love, Give, and Serve them but also how to do so much more.

"Wow!"

Yes, Anabeth. Truly wow!

CHAPTER 5: THE GIFT

Do you know what was happening for me at that very moment, Anabeth?

"Uh, I think so."

What do you think?

"I think you were being given a gift from God."

Exactly, Anabeth! That's correct. Being allowed to see deep into the heart and soul of a human being is something only God has the power to do. It is something He does to Love, Give, Serve, and connect with all His children in Heaven and on Earth. These are things we strive to do as Angels, but it is not always easy for us. Especially for a very new Angel-in-Training, like I was at the time.

Initially, I had been so worried about meeting God that I didn't see things clearly. I didn't realize that I was there in the elevator, at that exact moment, to serve a purpose. You see, while I was busy praying for God to be with me, He was there already. He had been all along. I just didn't realize it. When I prayed for the others, God came to me through that wonderful gift. He showed me that I only needed to be open to receiving it, that I just had to surrender to the gift He gave and allow His work to flow through me. I would use the gift to show and give God's grace to everyone in the elevator … with a little Angelic wisdom to help it along.

God taught me in that instant that it was possible to be the Archangel I wanted to be. Just like Barachiel said, I had to believe in myself in order to achieve it.

"So that's how you became an Archangel?"

Not quite that easily, Anabeth. That was just the start.

As eye-opening as my prayer was for me, it didn't seem to have the same effect for everyone in the elevator.

Betty was once again the first to speak up. "That was a lovely prayer, Ezra. Thank you."

"You're quite welcome, Betty."

She continued, "I pray every day and go to church as often as I can. I just can't get there as much as I like. We used to attend mass regularly back when I had my family. Even with seven children, we still managed to get them to church on time, mostly. Still, my husband always complained that he never got to hear the first reading 'cause we never arrived until the second one. He thought he was being funny, but I always took it seriously. I knew the importance for my kids' education and still ask them to raise my grandbabies the same way."

"My family takes religious education very seriously as well, Betty," I said. "Thank you for sharing that."

Big John spoke next. "You the son of a preacher man, or something?"

"Not exactly," I admitted. "I just have a lot of experience praying."

He laughed. "Experience? At your age? You're too young to have a lot of experience at anything, ha-ha!"

I chuckled right along with him, thinking about the irony of my assumed age in his eyes versus how "old" I actually was compared to all of them.

"You're ancient!"

Yes, Anabeth. You're funny, and I guess I am.

Next, Eva gave me a warm smile of appreciation but didn't actually say anything at first.

Adam gave a similar smile and then spoke up. "Eva and I used to pray a lot more than we do nowadays. We both come from religious families and were married in a great big church wedding. Eva was such a beautiful bride that day, and she still is!"

"Thank you, honey!" Eva responded. "Yes, our wedding was very beautiful. It was at the church I grew up in, which made it special at the time."

"Special at the time ... but not special now?" I asked her.

She dropped her head and started to cry. I reached out my hand to touch her shoulder, but Adam clutched her tightly. "It's not you," he told me. "We just received some bad news earlier today."

I put my hands on each of their shoulders. "I'm very sorry. I will pray for you."

Adam pulled his head up slightly from Eva's and said, "Thank you, that's kind of you, Ezra."

Carly looked up from Jo, who had fallen asleep, and said to me, "Maybe you can pray that Jo will not cry and stay asleep. If she wakes up screaming, it's going to be hell in here."

"I'm sure she will be fine," I reassured her.

"Sure, she'll be fine as long as she has something to eat." Carly made a bit of a face. "I just gave her the last bottle of formula, so now it's all on me. I haven't been able to satisfy her yet. What am I going to do when it's time for her next feeding?"

I gave her a sympathetic look and said, "I don't have a lot of experience with babies, but I do know that they have a special place with God. Jesus loved little children the most while he was on Earth. He always wanted them near to him, as he loved their innocence and big hearts. I can tell Jo has a very big heart and loves you very much already, no matter how much milk you have."

Carly laughed. "You're sweet, Ezra."

I could tell Matt was watching Carly. I looked over at him asked, "You said Jo looks like your daughter, correct?"

"Yes, I said that."

"How old is your daughter?" I asked.

"Well, she's clearly not a little baby anymore," Matt informed me with a snort. "Look at me—I'm an old man!"

I could tell my question had made him uncomfortable, so I just laughed innocently at his outburst. This settled him down a bit. "I don't know how old she is," he admitted. "I think around thirty-five or thirty-six. She even has a daughter of her own, but I don't know any more than that."

"Do you have any other children?" I asked, trying to loosen him up a bit.

"No! Just the one daughter. Like I said before, I'm an old vet, and that's all there is to it."

"Well," I replied, "I'll add your daughter and granddaughter to my prayers."

"You can pray all you want, but that's not going to change anything."

"Change what?" I asked.

"Nothing, nothing," he muttered, waving me off. "Go bother someone else."

"Sure, Matt. I'll check back with you later."

"He didn't seem to like you very much."

Well, not yet he didn't, but he would.

Joshua had overheard my conversation with Matt and said, "I don't think he's much of a talker."

"You may be right," I responded.

"I think it's good to pray," Joshua added. "It's nice to share things and get them off your chest."

"Is that so?" I asked, watching him thoughtfully.

"Absolutely!" Joshua agreed with enthusiasm. "I always tell the guys at Big Brother that they need to get the kids to open up more, to share what's on their mind so we can learn more about them."

"That's pretty sound advice," I agreed.

"I think so," Joshua nodded. "I think the more we keep them talking, the better. That way they can't get inside their heads."

I cocked my head a little. "Inside their heads? What do you mean, Joshua?"

"I mean that if they have no one to talk to, they bottle it all up and hold it inside, and we don't want that. That's what I always did as a teenager."

"So, what do you do now?" I asked.

"Now? Now, I just worry about the kids instead of myself. I don't have time for that."

"There's always time to pray," I reminded him.

"I knew you would tell him that!"

Yes, you're right, Anabeth. It is one of my favorite sayings, I admit.

"So, what did Joshua have to say about that?"

He said, "Maybe for some people, but I'm always go, go, go. I'll try it sometime. Thanks, Ezra."

I could tell he didn't want to share anymore, so I turned my attention elsewhere.

Olivia was once again poking elevator buttons and checking her cell phone simultaneously but not having success with either. I made sure she knew I was watching and said, "Based on what Big John said earlier, I think we may be stuck here for a while."

She met my gaze, almost defiantly. "You may have accepted the situation, but I haven't. I don't plan on being stuck here all night. I'll find a solution. I'll get myself out of this elevator."

"That would be helpful to *all* of us," I responded.

She seemed slightly agitated by that. "Don't get me wrong, you all seem very nice. I just can't worry about everyone else. I need to take care of myself. I need to focus on *me*."

I knew she wasn't ready to hear what she really needed to, so I just nodded shortly and said nothing in response.

She continued, "I'm sure everyone else in here is having some of the same thoughts as me. That's what people do. They think of themselves first." I didn't answer; instead, I just smiled at her. "Don't worry, Ezra, you're a nice guy. I'll make sure you get out too," she concluded as she went back to her phone.

"I bet I know what you wanted to tell her!"

You probably do, Anabeth. Don't worry; we'll get to that later in my story.

Faith was sitting on the ground cross-legged right in front of us, so I sat down across from her in the same childlike fashion. "How are you doing with all this?" I asked.

She looked at me with a wan smile. "I'm okay, I guess. Just wish we weren't stuck."

"It's a fortunate and unfortunate situation at the same time," I replied.

"What do you mean, fortunate?" she asked with an incredulous look. "I only see being stuck in an elevator as unfortunate, for sure."

"I see your point, Faith. You can look at our situation as an unfortunate turn of events; the elevator got stuck, security has left for the day, and you don't know how long you will be here. You can also look at the fortunate side of things; you are not alone, you have met some very nice, interesting people, and Ezra is here to pray for you." I pointed to my chest with a half-silly grin on my face.

She giggled a little. "It was a nice prayer," she admitted. "I wish I could pray like you. I hear prayers like that at St. Joseph's all the time, but never from me! Others are always so much better at it."

"I'm sure you pray great, Faith!" I responded emphatically. "Besides, God hears all prayers just the same."

"I doubt that!" she responded quickly with an anxious look, then abruptly snapped out, "Even if he hears them, he doesn't always answer them!"

A surge of her emotions poured over me, and I knew she was going to a place that she didn't like in herself. Immediately, I tried to help. "I know how you feel, and I feel the same way sometimes," I consoled, trying to comfort her. "Even if I don't know whether God hears me or will answer my prayers, I still keep praying."

She looked at me with wide eyes. "Why?" she asked emphatically.

"I keep praying because it simply makes me feel better. It allows me to share with God what I can't share with anyone else."

"I guess that makes sense," she replied with some acceptance. "Maybe I'll try it. Thanks for the tip, Ezra."

"You're welcome, Faith. We can talk more later if you like."

"Okay! You're pretty easy to talk to," she admitted with a smile.

I could tell that I had made a brief, small connection with Faith, one that I planned to deepen later.

"Yep! I can tell that too."

I'm sure you can, Anabeth.

It may have been most apparent with Faith, but that was not the only connection I made in the elevator. I was bonding with each passenger in a unique and different way, planting the seeds with which I would grow the change needed within them. You see, Anabeth, I had seen deep into their hearts and souls and knew they needed my help. That was just the beginning. What I couldn't answer yet was: How deeply rooted did their struggles, fears, insecurities, and weaknesses go? Where exactly were they in their personal journey? How receptive would they be to what I had to say? How open would they be to change, and how was I going to impart that change? I had a lot of work to do and very little time to get it done.

"Better put that gift to work!"

Yes, Anabeth. That's exactly what I did.

The clock was ticking, so I had to get going. Luckily, God's wisdom—**"Failure to prepare is preparing to fail"**—was ringing in my ears. I knew I needed a solid plan, so I thought fast. I felt strongly about the lessons and wisdom I needed to share with each of them but needed the right way to share it. I decided to give each individual a bit of wisdom to start. As they gained acceptance, I would then share it in the larger setting with everyone. This way, I could ensure the greatest impact from each lesson.

"Sounds like a good plan. Did it work?"

You'll soon find out, Anabeth.

CHAPTER 6: SHOW GRATITUDE

As I continued to fine-tune my plan in my head, I knew that the order in which I unveiled everything would be key. I had ten clear areas I needed to address within the group that I knew could truly change their lives. From my initial conversations with my fellow elevator riders, I knew I could attach a lesson to the troubles of each one of them to make that lesson relevant. Once I gained traction with some of the easier challenges they faced, I could show that I had some knowledge and wisdom to offer. Then I could tackle some of their larger, deeper issues. I drew upon all of my training and decided on a good order to follow. I decided the first lesson to teach would be:

SHOW GRATITUDE

"Why did you want to start with that?"

Well, Anabeth, by teaching my elevator companions to **SHOW GRATITUDE** first, I felt I would create a solid foundation to build upon.

"Makes sense."

I thought so too, Anabeth. It was also right in line with the gift I was given from God. When I received the gift in the elevator, the very first thing I wanted to do was show God gratitude, so I thanked Him for giving me something so wonderful. I also wanted to **SHOW GRATITUDE** to God by using that gift for His intended purpose. It seemed the most logical starting point. Plus, it just so happened that to **SHOW GRATITUDE** was one of the first lessons I learned as an Angel-in-Training.

"Sounds like a curious coincidence to me."

It did to me as well, Anabeth. I saw it as another sign from God that I was beginning in the right place.

"So, which person did you to start with?"

Good question, Anabeth. There were a few different options for sure, but no Earthly soul in my current company resonated more with me than Carly.

Carly stood out as the perfect person to begin with because of her beautiful baby, Jo. She had a glaring example of who and what to **SHOW GRATITUDE** for, right there in the elevator with all of us. Jo provided an instant and constant reminder to her and everyone as we shared our time together. Even more importantly, Carly needed this lesson more than anyone else there.

Before I could start her down that path, I had to find out how she had gotten to this point in her life. I decided to focus on her first. The timing seemed perfect; everyone was taking time for themselves. Most were now sitting on the elevator floor quietly, and a few were resting.

Carly sat reclined in one corner of the elevator. She had made a makeshift bed for Jo out of some blankets, her jacket, and her baby bag. "It looks like Jo is sleeping like a little Angel," I remarked.

Carly looked up with a smile. "Yes, she is—for now. It usually isn't this easy. She is a very fussy baby. I'm up every couple of hours with her most nights. I thought for sure she wouldn't sleep in this environment, but here she is, passed out. I'm just glad she is sleeping contently and peacefully."

"She does look very peaceful," I agreed.

"It's a miracle that she can even get to that state because I'm never peaceful—more like frantic and all over the place most of the time. I'm basically a hot mess." She sighed.

"What makes you say that?" I asked.

She glanced away, looking melancholy. "Oh, Ezra, you don't want to know."

"Sure I do," I quickly replied before she could refuse.

"Let's see. Where do I start? I'm a twenty-six-year-old single mother with a three-month-old baby I didn't plan for. My parents don't want anything to do with Jo because they say I was irresponsible when I got pregnant—so she's totally my responsibility. I'm not 100 percent sure who her father is, so I can't get support there. My friends aren't any help either. They're more interested in partying than babies—and I wish I could be having fun right there with them. I'm basically all alone with a child I wasn't ready for. To top it all off, I'm not producing enough milk to feed her—which I know I already mentioned—but it just shows me that I wasn't meant to have a baby in the first place!"

Wow. It was apparent that Carly had a lot of emotions roiling inside, considering how quickly they had spilled out of her. I was glad that she felt comfortable opening up a little and knew I had to have a good response. "I don't think that's true at all," I began. "I know Jo is a wonderful gift from God and one of the most special blessings you can receive."

Carly offered a slightly uplifted smile. "You really believe that?"

"Absolutely!" I responded emphatically. "Do you remember what I said earlier when you asked me to pray for Jo?"

"Yes, you said something about children having a special place with God."

"That's exactly correct. God loves all of His children, especially the little ones."

"How do you know?" she asked, brow furrowed.

"He told me, of course!"

My response clearly caught her off guard, and I chuckled to myself. *If she only knew ….*

"Huh?" she finally asked.

"In the Bible, of course," I told her. "It says so in the Bible."

She half-rolled her eyes at me, as if I'd just given her a major cop-out, and then said, "If that's true, then why doesn't God make it easier? Why don't I know what to do with Jo? Why did I have a baby I wasn't ready for?"

I softened my tone, placed my hand on Jo, and said, "All of these are valid questions, and they all have meaning to you, or else you wouldn't have asked them. Unfortunately, I can't answer them, because they don't have meaning for me. I don't see any of the things you question as problems. I see them all as opportunities and blessings!"

Carly's eyes widened for a second, then her face scrunched back up in confusion. "I think I understand … but I'm not sure. What do you mean exactly?"

"I mean that what you see as problems, I see as opportunities because we have a different mindset. You are viewing your issues from a negative mindset, while I am viewing them from a positive one. Think glass half-empty versus glass half-full."

"Okay," she said slowly. "That makes some sense. I know I can get negative when things get difficult. But even If I could look at things more positively, that won't make them easier."

"You're right!" I agreed with a smile. "It won't make them easier, and you don't want that anyway."

"But I do!" she retorted ardently.

"No!" I blurted out in my *teacher* voice.

"I know that tone!"

Yes, Anabeth, I'm sure you do, and Carly was going to learn too.

"No, Carly." I shook my head. "You don't actually want things to be easier. What you really want is to be better, stronger … more prepared."

Her eyes once again swelled, so I continued. "Those so-called problems are all opportunities you have, each and every moment you spend with Jo, and will allow you to grow as a mother and provider for your baby."

"So how can I get there?" she whispered. "How can I get to the place where I see them the same way you do?"

I smiled, again placing my hand on her shoulder, and said, "That, Carly, is the simple part."

Her puzzled look returned, and she stared at me silently.

"To 'get there,' as you say, you only need to do one thing."

"What?" she asked, her voice desperate and pleading. "What do I have to do?"

I straightened and said, "**SHOW GRATITUDE.**"

"**SHOW GRATITUDE?**" she parroted back blankly.

"That's it. By Showing Gratitude for Jo and the wonderful blessing and gift that she is, you will automatically change your mindset to a positive one and shift your thinking. You will automatically see 'problems' as opportunities. Gratitude is the magic that has been missing in your life with Jo."

Carly's face changed. I could see the emotional transformation overtake her, and tears glistened in her eyes. She picked up Jo to hold her close. "I can't believe that I haven't been grateful for her, or how I could be so selfish. How couldn't I have realized this before?"

"Don't place any blame on yourself, Carly," I offered in my most comforting tone. "You have done the best you possibly could with Jo. You have focused on feeding her, changing diapers, and caring for her. You just didn't have time to stop and think about it. The great news is that she is still very young. You have your whole life to **SHOW GRATITUDE** for her, and she will in turn show it for you as well."

Carly nodded, brushing away a tear. "I want that. I want to show her how grateful I am for her and how much she means to me."

"Then do so," I said matter-of-factly. "Make a commitment, then express it with your actions. Your belief of it will increase until it permeates your whole being. By changing your attitude to one of gratitude, you will see your life change in many ways."

"What kind of ways, Ezra?"

"Positive ones!"

Carly was visibly shaken by what I had said so far, but I knew I would still need to dig further within her. It was clear that many of her behaviors were rooted deep into her past. Carly wiped her eyes again and then said, "Ezra, you're a nice guy, and I don't know how old you are, but you're probably wiser than your age. Anyway, how can I trust you? How do I know all of this will really work? It can't be this easy."

I looked her straight in the eyes as I reverted back to teacher mode. "It will not be easy."

"But you said—"

"What I said was that the solution was simple," I interrupted. "I never said it would be easy."

"Same thing!" she exclaimed with the impudence of a defiant child.

"Not exactly. Let me explain. To get where you need to go, you must **SHOW GRATITUDE**. This is, in essence, the 'simple' solution to your problem. It is the destination you need to reach to be in a better place than you are now. The questions, doubts, and fears—which you can consider as the 'baggage'—are the same ones you have always had. This baggage is a part of you and always will be until you change it or learn to make it work to your benefit."

"Okay, I understand. I have a lot of baggage. My ex-boyfriend used to tell me that all the time." she said in a dejected tone.

"Look, Carly," I said firmly, "whether you have 'baggage' or not isn't what's important. What's important is how you use it. Will you continue to let it drag you down and keep you from growing, or utilize it to propel you to places you've never been?"

"I want to use it in a good way. I don't like being selfish, and I definitely don't want Jo to grow up with the same baggage that I have," she told me.

"See! You're making progress already!" I practically shouted with joy, startling the others around us. "That is a very positive statement and could only come from a grateful heart. You are on the right track toward Showing Gratitude."

"Great! The right track is what I want for Jo and myself. So how do I stay on the Gratitude track toward my new destination?" she said with a sly smile, showing that she had been listening.

"You stay there by putting in the work. This is what I meant when I said the solution is simple but will not be easy. I can give you some tips, but it will take constant, conscious effort on your part to stay there."

"Tips are good. I can definitely use some," Carly responded with enthusiasm.

"Outstanding!" I said with a matching amount of gusto.

"Do you by any chance have a journal?" Carly's eyes gleamed with interest. "I did when I was a teenager but stopped writing in it a few years ago. Now I mainly just use social media to journal my life."

"Okay. Do you think you get as much out of social media as you did when you wrote in your journal?"

She thought for a moment. "Honestly? Probably not. I feel that social media is for everyone else, whereas my journal was just for me. I never shared it with anyone."

"So, you tended to use your journal for writing more intimate things, more for your thoughts and feelings?"

"Yes, it was definitely more personal," Carly shared.

I nodded. "It seems so by what you're saying. How do you feel about writing like you used to in your journal?"

"I'd like that. I always enjoyed it and felt good after I wrote in it." Her lips spread in a big grin.

"Perfect!" I said with approval. "Start by writing down all the things you are grateful for, no matter how big or small. Take your list and keep it where you can see it each morning and night, like in your journal on the nightstand. You can even hang it on the bathroom mirror where you take all your selfies!"

"You said that! How Earthly modern of you. Lol."

Yes, Anabeth. I can be cool sometimes. Carly laughed when I said it too.

I continued to make recommendations to Carly. "Read through your list every day at least once and take the time to reflect on the various things you are grateful for. Write down in your journal the additional new things you are grateful for each day. As you get more comfortable with the process, you can journal your thoughts on things you have yet to **SHOW GRATITUDE** for but want to. Once you start to form a habit of this behavior, it will reinforce your ability to show gratitude in all areas of your life. Remember what I said earlier: Make a commitment, then express it with your actions, and then your belief of it will increase until it permeates your whole being."

Carly's shoulders slumped in relief. "That sounds like exactly what I need."

"Beautiful! I think it will help you out significantly. There's just one more important component to add that will make Showing Gratitude work."

"What's that?" Carly asked with anticipation.

"God!" I responded with resounding belief. "God is the single most important part. He will make sure all this change takes root within your heart. He will be there to constantly water and nurture it to make it grow, to help you enjoy the benefits of your efforts."

"But I'm not that religious. I haven't been to church since I was young, and I only pray to God when things aren't going well in my life."

"That's okay, Carly," I replied supportively. "Sure, God is a part of all of these things, but He's a lot more too. You said you liked my prayer earlier, so let's keep it simple and start there. When is the last time you prayed?"

"With you. A couple hours ago," she admitted with a giggle.

I laughed. "Okay, yes. I mean before that."

"Well, I don't remember exactly when, but I know I prayed a lot when I first got pregnant."

"And what did you pray for?"

"I don't know. A lot of things. I prayed that I was doing the right thing by keeping Jo and that she would be healthy.

I prayed that I would know what to do when she was born. Stuff like that."

"Okay, and how did you feel when you prayed?"

"Good, I guess."

"Do you think it helped?" I asked.

"I think so."

"Let's look at it another way," I suggested. "Did praying give you some of the same feelings that writing in your journal did?"

"Yes, yes, it did! It made me feel like I had gotten something off my chest so I wouldn't have to keep it to myself."

"I'm very glad to hear that, Carly," I told her with excitement. "This clearly shows that God is a part of your life already. He is and has always been there, whether you knew it or not."

She looked surprised. "Really?"

"Yes, Carly! God is there for you anytime you need Him. You simply need to accept His love and let Him into your heart."

"And will I let Him into my heart if I start to **SHOW GRATITUDE** for Jo and other things in my life?"

"Absolutely!" I shouted joyously, as if I had just struck gold. "You see? Simple. If you need a little help opening your heart to God, you can start by reciting a very short verse about gratitude from **Psalm 118:1: 'Give thanks to the Lord, for he is good; his love endures forever.'**"

"I can do that!" she said with mounting excitement.

"That's great, Carly!"

Carly paused for a minute to hug Jo. The young mother

looked as if she was soaking it all in as she rocked her little one back and forth. She stopped moving to signify she had gone through it all in her head and looked up. "Ezra?"

"Yes, Carly?" I asked with anticipation.

"I'm ready. I'm ready to change, to put in the work. I'm ready to **SHOW GRATITUDE**, and most important, I'm ready to open my heart to God!"

"Yay! Woo-hoo!"

Yes, Anabeth. I thought the same thing at the time. Carly's words were so heartfelt and emphatic that they took me by surprise. I couldn't believe I had taken her so far in such a short period of time. I had gotten her to the place she needed to be. I had dug deep into the problems I had seen inside her heart and found a solution that she willingly accepted. It was as if I had practiced my own miracle. Instead of jumping up and down and celebrating—which I wanted to do—I just stood there frozen, as I had been earlier in the elevator, and soaked her emotions in like a sponge.

An eternity seemed to pass, though in actuality it was probably only a couple seconds, until I broke my statue-like state and yelled out, *"Amen! A big Amen to that, Carly!"*

She laughed at my silliness and then pulled me over to join in a group hug with her and Jo. As we embraced, I could feel emotions pouring out of Carly like beams of light across the sky, all of it just as intense as it had previously felt—though now I was able to absorb it into my heart and soul without hesitation. Many emotions swirled around in her, to be sure, but one emotion shined brighter than the rest, like a beacon in the night. It was pure Gratitude.

"I can feel Gratitude right now as you describe it!"

Yes, Anabeth. I feel it too.

Our hug had woken Jo, so Carly proceeded to change her diaper and feed her. She took out another blanket to cover herself and began without hesitation. She had a resounding confidence that emanated from her motherly nurturing. She looked down at Jo with a look of tenderness and love, whispering softly to her as she stroked her head and back with the caress only a mother can deliver. I couldn't make out what she was saying but could still feel her expressing Gratitude for Jo with each tender touch.

CHAPTER 7: BE PRESENT

Fortunately, my conversation with Carly did not go unnoticed by others. Not everyone was actively paying attention to us, but some glanced over now and then during our conversation. While I wasn't purposefully trying to include or exclude them, I did want them to get a feel for what was going on. As I said, early success with one person was crucial to planting seeds of inquisition in others. I needed them to see that I had some wisdom to offer and be open to asking for and receiving it.

"I bet everyone at least heard the Amen!"

Yes, Anabeth. That's correct. My Amen was so loud that it woke everyone up, and I don't just mean the people who were actually sleeping.

Matt was clearly startled the most. "You gonna be that loud all night? I was trying to sleep," He grumbled like a child not wanting to wake up for school.

"Sorry, Matt," I offered kindly. "I get a little excited about stuff like this."

"Stuff like what, religion?" he asked with a hint of disdain.

"Yes, religion does excite me, but that's not what I mean. I get excited about spending time helping others."

"Ha! I doubt it." Matt shrugged. "People always say that, but they don't really mean it. Most people are only interested in being fake-nice."

"Fake-nice?" I repeated, puzzled.

"You know, phony. Most people pretend they care when they really don't. They just do it because they want something for themselves."

I chuckled a little for the sake of politeness but didn't quite agree with what he was saying.

He offered a patronizing grin, showing teeth badly in need of a dentist's care. "Ezra, you're young and probably a bit naïve to this world. Me, on the other hand, I've been a lot of places and seen a lot. Trust me. I know what I'm talking about."

"It sounds like you have had some less than ideal relation-ships with others," I mentioned, hoping to encourage him to open up more."

"Less than ideal? That's one way to put it. Let's just say, I learned a long time ago that the only one you can trust to be there when you need him is yourself. If you rely on others you are just asking to be disappointed."

"That sounds like a really lonely place to be," I commented with a sad smile.

"Ha! Maybe so, but it's a place I'm familiar with—and a place I choose to be."

I could feel Matt growing defensive, and I paused. There had to be a way to meet him on common ground. I nodded slowly to stay connected with him, though I didn't accept his comments as wholly honest.

Luckily, Carly had just finished feeding Jo when she must have overheard Matt. She looked up at us. "You mentioned you had a daughter like Jo once," she said, gesturing at Matt. "She's all done nursing. Would you like to burp her?"

Matt was clearly thrown off by Carly's offer but seemed moderately touched at the same time. Carly extended Jo toward Matt, making it difficult for him to say no. "Here, please take her. My arms are getting tired, and I can use the break."

Matt took Jo cautiously but without any hesitation. He held her up to his shoulder and began swaying, offering the familiar, rhythmic back-pats of a seasoned grandfather. "How's this?" he asked.

Carly smiled. "That's just how she likes it."

Matt's disposition had softened by virtue of Carly's interjection, so I took the opportunity to get him to open up again. I smiled in affirmation of his actions and said, "Looks like you've done that before."

"A little" he admitted, lifting one shoulder in a slight shrug.

He wasn't budging with me. Luckily, Carly again took the lead. "How long has it been since you held a little one?" she inquired.

"A loooong, long time. Not since my daughter Hope was little, like Jo. I used to help my ex-wife with holding Hope after she fed her. I wasn't much for changing diapers, but I always enjoyed holding her after she ate. She was just so peaceful." Matt's tone and expression softened as he spoke.

"I know what you mean," replied Carly. "I love the closeness I feel when I hold Jo while she's sleeping. It's just pure tranquility." She held one hand up to her heart. "Did it used to give you the same type of feelings, Matt?"

Matt pondered for a quick second and then nodded. "Yep, that's it. That's what I enjoyed about it too. It was just so different from the hostility and violence of my usual world that I found it comforting." He seemed to fade away for a minute, lost in thought, then continued, "Sometimes it was the only quiet I experienced in a whole month."

"That must have been challenging," Carly said, her voice thick with sympathy.

"Maybe, but I never really thought about it back then. I was too busy being a soldier and doing my job. I didn't have time to get too soft with babies," Matt finished, his voice growing gruff again as he tried to resume his strong exterior.

I could feel that Matt was on the verge of really going somewhere, if he would just let go a little bit. Carly seemed to feel it too; I could tell she wanted to help learn more about him. What both of us didn't realize was that Jo apparently felt it as well.

"Huh? How did you know Jo felt it? She's just a baby."

Patience, Anabeth. I'm getting there. Just when Matt was about to retreat into his comfortable bunker, devoid of any obvious vulnerability or tenderness, Jo let out a loud burp and nuzzled her head against Matt's shoulder.

That little eruption out of Jo's mouth was more powerful than any enemy attack Matt had experienced, and he found himself powerless against it. He nuzzled his head against hers. "There you go, little baby," he murmured. "That's it." Carly smiled widely and gave Matt a tender pat on the shoulder.

"Go on, Matt. Go and enjoy the tranquility. There are no more wars to wage here, no more battles to fight. Take the time to enjoy the peace."

Matt's eyes began to tear up slightly. Carly had obviously struck a chord. "I wish I had the time you're talking about, Carly," he said sadly. "Unfortunately, my time is almost up."

"Almost up?" I inquired, sliding back into their conversation. "What do you mean?"

"I mean exactly what I said, Ezra. My time is almost up."

I knew exactly what Matt meant. I had felt it earlier but wanted him to share it with Carly. If he could find the strength to be vulnerable, his heart would finally open fully. Once that happened, he would be ready to receive some help.

Carly was clearly still riding the high of emotions from our intimate conversation as she took Matt's hand in hers. "It's okay, Matt," she began. "You're not alone anymore. We're right here." She reached out with her other hand and clasped mine. "Tell us what you really mean, Matt."

Matt's eyes were glistening. He looked around to make sure no one else was paying attention and then confessed, "I'm dying. My doctor just gave me the news today. My latest test results came back—my cancer has metastasized. There are no more treatments that will help. He gave me two months."

Carly's eyes also held a sheen of welling tears as she absorbed this tragic news. She smiled at Matt and said, "I really, really want to hug you right now. Is that okay?"

Matt didn't speak; he just nodded and moved toward Carly to accept her tender gesture.

She hugged him tightly, filing a massive void that had engulfed his heart throughout the years of solitude.

Matt accepted her hug willingly, closing his eyes and smiling. It was almost as if, in that moment, she was a surrogate for the daughter he wished were there.

I observed all of this as I opened myself to the emotions they exchanged.

Carly's kindness had done it—it proved to be the key that opened the door to Matt's real self, the self that lay beyond the gruff exterior. It was my turn now …. I had to step inside the depths of Matt's challenges to help where I could.

Matt and Carly had broken off their embrace but remained close together, still basking in the light of the love they had both felt. I knew Matt's acceptance of Jo was my way in. I began there.

"It looks like the best medicine for you right now is more family time, Matt," I told him.

He looked at me incredulously. "That may be true, Ezra, but how am I supposed to make that happen? I haven't seen my daughter in years, let alone my granddaughter. She probably couldn't even pick me out of a lineup."

Carly responded before I could even gather a thought. "You start by taking one small step at a time, Matt. That's it. Don't worry about the destination. Just focus on the first step of the journey." She looked at me with confidence and for approval.

I smiled and winked at her with a nod. She was doing a perfect job of passing along the message I had taught her.

Carly straightened her shoulders and turned back to Matt.

"Matt, I can say with 100 percent certainty that every daughter has a special place for their father in their heart. I'm sure Hope has reserved such a spot for you, and she's just waiting for the day you come back into her life to fill it."

Matt's weathered eyes had turned into mini faucets as the tears fell, his crow's feet carrying them down his face like tiny aqueducts. He tried to compose himself. "I'd like to think that she has that seat saved for me, but how can I know? What if she won't see me? What if she wants nothing to do with me?"

Carly's face clouded over as she struggled to find answers to Matt's challenging questions. So, I went for the opening. "Matt, the answer to those questions does not reside within Hope, it resides within you."

"What does that mean?" he asked as he hastily wiped his tears away to make sure no one else noticed them.

"How would you answer those questions for her? What does your heart tell you?"

"Well, like I said, I'd like to think she does. I'd like to think she would want to see me and let me meet my granddaughter." Some of the harsh lines seemed to melt as hope brightened his features.

"Then you have your answer," I responded with my usual teacher know-how.

Matt still wasn't sold, though. "Let's say that you're right, Ezra. Let's say my heart is on target, and she feels the same way. You're saying the only way to know for sure is to take a chance and find out?"

"That's correct, Matt. It's the only way to be 100 percent certain."

Matt's eyes fell to the carpeting. "Sounds like I could be setting myself up for big disappointment if it doesn't go well."

"That's true as well, Matt," I agreed.

"Not very reassuring, are you, Ezra?" he grumbled, sounding like an impetuous teenager.

"Nothing is certain, Matt. That's true in not just this situation, but with everything in life. You never know exactly what is going to happen until you act. It is only by actually following your heart and taking action that you get to the outcome … whatever it may be."

Matt rubbed his chin. "Sounds risky. I've always preferred to keep my distance from everyone and everything. That way, I don't have to get too involved."

Or too hurt, I thought to myself. I knew that was what this was all about. By not getting involved, he didn't have to worry about taking any emotional damage.

"Yes, Matt. That's the familiar and lonely place you described earlier. That's where you've resided most of your life, isn't it?"

"I guess." He rolled his shoulders in a defeated shrug, slumping over a little.

Carly once again put her hand on his shoulder to offer comfort.

I continued, "You also said you wished you had more time to spend with the ones you love. Well, now is the time to do it. Take that chance and cherish every moment with them."

"That seems nice, and I would really love to see them," he said, though still with a lingering tone of uncertainty.

I could tell Matt was getting close but needed a big push—and in a way that he felt familiar with. "Matt, when you were a soldier, you were probably good at taking orders."

He suddenly beamed and stood up a little straighter. "The best!"

"Okay. And when you were given orders, did you have much time to debate them and think about the 'what ifs?'"

"No. Never. We had to live in the moment and act."

"Perfect!" I exclaimed. "That's all I am asking you to do now. The only order you need to follow now is to **BE PRESENT.**"

"**BE PRESENT**?" he questioned.

"Yes Matt, Being Present is what you need to focus on for the rest of your life. This will allow you to live and—more importantly—love in every moment you have left. It will allow you to live each day as if it were your last, because it very well may be."

Carly looked a little taken aback at the force of my words and tone, but I knew it was the best approach with Matt—a drill sergeant relaying orders to a lifelong soldier.

I didn't let up and barked, "Matt, you don't have the luxury of wasting any time on this mission! It needs your full attention right away. What are you going to do about it, Matt?"

Matt's veins were protruding at the temples, as if all the blood had rushed to his head in anger. His clenched fists shouted loud and clear that he didn't like being challenged by little old me, but he said nothing. So, I pressed on, "Look,

Matt, maybe I'm not being clear. To **BE PRESENT** means that you will not think about yourself but those you are with. You will put them first and make sure you are supporting them!"

"You don't have to explain anymore!" Matt roared. "I know what it means. I did that all the time in the Marines!"

"Great! So, what are you going to do about it, now, *soldier*?" I hollered, poking him rapid-fire in the chest.

"**BE PRESENT**! *Sir*!" he exclaimed, stiff and arrow-straight, as if standing at attention at the foot of a freshly made bunk. "I'm going to go see my daughter and granddaughter and be present with them for all the days I have left!" he yelled out, though the strength of his words was overtaken by the naked emotion on his face.

Carly once again grabbed Matt, folded him into her arms, and held him tightly. He sank his head into her shoulder, as Jo did in his, and wept in her arms the way a child would feeling the consolation only a mother could provide. It was a lot for him to share, let go, and commit to, all at once. So great was the emotional and physical toll of this experience that Matt did not move for about five minutes or so. Carly stood strong the whole time, consoling and providing the comfort he had longed for his whole life.

When Matt had recovered somewhat, he whispered, "Thank you," to Carly and then looked toward me with a face of stone. In one broad step, he bridged the distance between us, standing right in front of me. He snapped his feet together and drew his face toward mine until it was close enough for me to read read every fierce crease and age line that a hard life had etched upon it.

Matt thrust his index finger at my chest. "You … you got a lot of nerve for a kid, pushing an old Marine like that!"

I was slightly frightened but didn't back down. I needed to make sure my point stuck with him. "Matt, I—"

Matt reached out and pulled me in for a huge hug. "Get over here, you wannabe drill sergeant." And with that, he squeezed the breath out of me. "It takes guts to do what you just did, and I appreciate it. No one has called me out like that since I was a private. I know I'm a stubborn old S.O.B., but I guess this old dog can still learn a trick or two."

His embrace overflowed with strong, genuine emotions. Gratitude, love, trust, and some remorse poured out of him, but most of all, I felt Matt's heart, mind, and soul, right there with me. He had heard the message and was prepared to take action right away. I was proud of him. As we broke our hug, I kept a hold of his right arm. "Matt, I'm just glad that we were able to **BE PRESENT** here with one another to accept this gift."

"What gift?" he probed.

"The gift of each other's presence right here, right now, in this elevator. Our time together is truly a gift from God that I am very grateful for."

Carly stood in support of my words. "I'm grateful for meeting you both too! I'm also grateful that you helped me care for Jo, Matt, and that you shared some of your burden with us."

Matt extended his other arm toward Carly, so he was now touching each of us in a circle. "Thank you both. I am grateful that I can **BE PRESENT** with both of you. I kind of like how this feels. I really want to **BE PRESENT** with Hope and my granddaughter too, if I can."

"You will!" I immediately responded with 100-percent certainty. Before Matt could question me, I added, "I can tell you're still feeling a little anxious about all of this, right?"

Matt nodded.

"Since God gave us this gift, you just need to ask him to support you in being present with Hope and your granddaughter. I know if you ask for his help, He will hear your prayers.

"How do you know?" The old soldier obviously wasn't completely convinced yet.

"Matt, God is always there to help you. You only need to be open to receiving it. Just as you allowed us to help you."

I could tell Matt was still dealing with the internal conflict that had plagued him his whole life. "I pretty much stopped praying when I entered the military. I saw too many bad things and felt it wasn't worth it."

I interrupted to keep his mounting negativity at bay. "It's always worth it, Matt, if you believe that God is there to help."

Carly interjected, "I was skeptical too, but I can tell you now—it's worth it."

"Okay," Matt replied with half-confidence.

"Look, Matt, I know you've been used to taking orders for most of your life. Well, the Bible is full of 'orders' for you to follow on this topic. One of my favorites is **Philippians 4:6: 'Do not be anxious about anything, but in everything by prayer and supplication with thanksgiving let your requests**

be made known to God.' You see, Matt, by thanking God for helping you to **BE PRESENT**, you are praying for His support with your family. There is no need to be anxious because God is with you."

Matt smiled widely. "Those are the types of orders I can stand behind. I mean, I want to make sure my remaining time is as good as it can be, so it's worth a shot."

Both Carly and I smiled in support as I emphasized, "We're proud of you, Matt. Your heart is in the right place. It's right here, present with us. As long as you continue to **BE PRESENT** with those you love, it won't matter how much time you have left, because you will have all the time you need."

Matt stood straight up at attention and saluted me as if I were a five-star general and then thanked Carly and me. He was now where he needed to be in order to live the rest of his remaining life to the fullest. He sat back down, settling in one corner of the elevator as he tried to get some much-needed rest.

CHAPTER 8: GROW

"*Looks like you were off to a good start.*"

Yes, Anabeth. I thought so.

"*Who did you help next?*"

When I was ready, I helped the one who needed it most.

"*You're being a little vague, there, Teacher.*"

What I mean is that being in the elevator so close with everyone was very draining for me. I had just expended a lot of energy feeling their emotions, so I opted to pray and meditate for a few minutes. No sooner had I leaned against the wall and closed my eyes that I felt a tug on my sleeve. I opened my eyes to reveal a very anxious-looking Percy.

Even after I opened my eyes Percy kept tugging on my sleeve like a five-year-old wanting a cookie. "Yes, Percy," I replied, which stopped the tugging. "How can I help you?"

Percy had apparently mustered up just enough courage to come over to me, but it had so emotionally strained him that he seemed to have already forgotten why. "Uh, um, I-I-I wanted to ask you something."

"Go ahead, Percy. I'm listening."

"Um, I couldn't help but overhear some of your conversation with ... with ...." He hung on the word as if it were the final piece of a hangman puzzle and he knew he was about to lose.

"You mean Matt?" I volunteered helpfully.

"Yes, but keep your voice down," he hissed, glancing around. "I don't want him to know I'm talking about him."

"Don't worry. Matt is pretty tired, so he's getting some rest. I know we're probably all tired, myself included." I really did want to help him, but I let that last part slip in the hope that he'd give me the opportunity to take a break to pray for a bit.

Percy was undaunted. "I can tell that you helped him and also the lady with the baby."

"Carly."

"Yes, Carly. I saw you talking to her too. You must be a good listener," he said, an eager gleam in his eyes.

"I try my best, Percy, and I really enjoy helping others, which makes it easier for me."

"I'm pretty shy, so I don't talk to others much. Mainly just my cat at night, but he never responds." He capped off that comment with a slightly lopsided grin.

I chuckled obligingly to help put him at ease. "Well, I'm happy to speak with you now, Percy. Hopefully, I have more to offer than your cat. What's on your mind?"

Percy paused to observe everyone else, who were in various states of rest since it was now after 11 p.m. He focused back on me and said, "Something caught my attention in your prayer. You said that being stuck in the elevator is an opportunity to make friends and have a new experience."

"Yes, Percy. That's part of what I said."

He shifted his weight restlessly. "Did you say that just to calm everyone down? To make us feel better 'cause we all realized we were stuck?"

"Not at all, Percy. I used those words in my prayer because I truly believe them."

"You do?"

"Yes, I wholeheartedly believe that we were meant to be here together at this moment in time."

Percy's eyes had dilated to cat-level. Clearly, he was a little uncomfortable with my viewpoint, so I scaled back. "How do you feel about our situation, Percy?"

"Not like that!" he blurted out. "Anything but that. Let's see, at first, I felt scared, then anxious, then restless, then uncomfortable, and now I'm tired."

"That's a variety of emotions," I said, mimicking a politician's business-like demeanor so as to not assign judgment to any of his words.

"I always have a lot of emotions if I don't keep a close eye on them or forget to take my medication ...." His jaw wobbled, and he glanced up at me in a mild panic. "Oops, I shouldn't have told you that. Please don't tell the others."

"Don't worry, Percy. Everything we share will be just between the two of us," I replied in a more sincere and less political tone.

"Good, because I don't want anyone to think I'm weird, or anything."

"I highly doubt anybody in here will think that," I reassured.

"Don't be so sure, Ezra. People say I'm weird all the time. Wait, your name is Ezra, right?" he asked as if he knew the answer but wanted reassurance anyway.

"Yes, Percy, I'm Ezra. You have it right. What else do you want to talk about?"

"I-I want to know how I can be more like you." He stared at me with big, hopeful eyes.

"Like me? I'm not sure I understand what you mean, Percy."

Percy took a deep breath and then exhaled his words as if he blowing up a big balloon. "What I mean is that you seem so confident. So sure of yourself. You got us all to pray with you and didn't hesitate at all, even after the old lady gave you water when it looked like you were going to get sick, you just snapped out of it. I could never assert myself like that. I think I would have puked right then and there if everyone were staring at me."

I did my best not to laugh at the vision of what Percy puking would look like. "Percy, I can assure you I was terrified at that exact moment too. I didn't know what I was going to say or do either. It may have seemed like I snapped out of it to you, but to me, it felt like I struggled for an eternity."

"Oh! I know what struggling like that feels like! I feel like that all the time!" Percy replied eagerly, like a second-grader who knew the answer to the problem written on the chalkboard. "That's what I'm talking about. How do I get better about not feeling that way?"

"Teacher, where did you even start?"

Percy clearly had a lot running through his mind, Anabeth.

I figured the best place to start was to share what worked for me.

"Well, Percy," I began, "seeing as we can relate in terms of our anxiety, I'll share what I do in anxious times, like the ones we experienced earlier."

"Okay. Please. I want to know," he said with mounting excitement.

"Anytime I don't have the answer, I simply pray," I explained.

"You pray?" His expression grew incredulous. "That's it?"

"Yes Percy, that's it. I know it sounds like I'm oversimplifying, so let me explain."

"Yeah, you're going to have to, 'cause I need more details than just 'I Pray,'" Percy insisted with slightly rolled eyes.

Calmly, I continued, "Whenever I get stuck in a situation that I can't control and feel like I don't have the answer or am scared of what will happen next, I take a moment to pause and ask God to help me **GROW** through the experience."

"What do you mean, **GROW**? How does that help?" Percy asked, slightly agitated and exasperated at the same time.

I considered for a moment, then said, "Look at it this way, Percy. Every time you get in a challenging or uncomfortable situation, what do you usually do?"

"I freeze or run from it as fast as I can," he replied firmly.

"All right. And does it get any easier to deal with the next time?"

"*No*! it definitely doesn't. Mostly it gets worse. It seems like each time is harder than the last." Percy looked suddenly hopeless and lost.

I smiled with understanding and nodded. "That's exactly what I figured you would say because I used to feel the same way. It wasn't until I decided to face my fears that things started to improve. Once I made a conscious effort to **GROW** from each experience, things began to get better for me."

"So, how did you **GROW**?"

"In lots of ways, Percy, and I continue to **GROW** each day. When you face your fears or challenge yourself, when you force yourself to be uncomfortable, you allow growth to take place."

Percy rubbed his hands together, looking uncertain. "But isn't it hard at the same time?"

"Yes, it can be, but it gets easier." I met his anxious stare with confidence. "Look at it this way. Were you always the accountant that you are today?"

"Oh, no. When I was younger, I made a lot of errors in my calculations. I had to re-do my work all the time."

"So how about now?"

"Now, my numbers are extremely accurate. I rarely ever make mistakes." His mouth twitched up, hinting at a proud smile.

"Precisely!" I met his shadow of a smile with a broad grin. "You had to **GROW** in your abilities to be the accountant that you are today. It wasn't overnight, but over time, things became less challenging as your skills improved and grew."

Percy still looked a little like a man grappling with an unfinished jigsaw puzzle, but he seemed to be getting there, so I broke it down further. "Look, Percy, I know you said that you like being comfortable and not changing, but if you want to improve, assert yourself when things get challenging, and gain confidence, you're going to have to put yourself in difficult and uncomfortable situations."

Percy flinched back a little. "That sounds really scary!"

"You're right. It will be, the first time, but the second will be a little easier, and the third easier than that, and so on. Before you know it, you will hardly notice the fear any longer. It will just be an insignificant round-up to the calculations from your past."

Percy chuckled at my attempt at an accounting reference. "That's your secret, huh?"

"Yes Percy, that's my secret. That's what has worked for me and what I'm sure will work for you too."

Percy took a seat on the floor and motioned for me to do the same. He paused and slowly closed his eyes, doing his best to mimic my earlier behavior as he processed the calculations needed for his own solution in his head. His behavior told me I had made some traction and now needed to dig in to seed more growth in the right direction.

"Okay, Ezra. I understand that in order to improve I will need to allow myself to **GROW**. I also get that it may be challenging and uncomfortable. What I still don't get is what does God and praying have to do with it."

"Everything, Percy!"

"*Everything*?" He shook his head. "Look, Ezra, I'm more spiritual than religious. I guess I pray sometimes, but I really think it's more like meditation. My therapist is working with me on it to help with my anxiety."

"That's great, Percy! I love meditation too."

"So, when I pray, I'm just supposed to ask God to help me **GROW,** and voila?" He raised his arms dramatically.

"Not exactly, Percy. Yes, God is there to help you along the way. He will support you, and having him in your heart will make the tough times easier, but God is not going to pull a rabbit out of a hat for you. If you pray to **GROW**, He will not give you growth. He will give you opportunities to **GROW** and provide situations you can learn from. He will help you become stronger and better equipped to handle things the next time. Scripture tells us in **John 15:5: 'I am the vine; you are the branches. If you remain in me and I in you, you will bear much fruit; apart from me you can do nothing.'** With God's help, you can **GROW** far greater than you can on your own."

"That makes a little sense, Ezra. Is that why you called our time an opportunity?"

"Yes, Percy! That's exactly what I was thinking when I prayed for all of us. By viewing our time together as an opportunity, we open our minds to the potential for growth. We prime the pump, so to speak—or in your case, do the initial calculations to forecast the future."

Percy once again chuckled. "That's not quite how the process works in accounting, but I understand the analogy, Ezra."

I shook my head at my own cheesiness.

"Yeah, that was pretty cheesy."

Yes, Anabeth, I know.

Percy closed his eyes and put his hands on his knees as if fashioning a meditative state. He sat there for a couple of minutes and then looked at me with a newfound look of strength. "All my life, I have thought that by taking the easy road I was doing myself a favor. By not challenging myself and not taking risks, I would be content. I now see that I have been selling myself short all along. The road I have been on was not smooth because it was the right path, it was smooth because it had a layer of boredom on top. I'm ready to get off that road and move on. I'm ready to be uncomfortable and challenge myself. I'm ready to **GROW!**" Percy took a deep breath and exhaled it, calm and confidant, smiling fully.

"Amen, Percy! That's great! I can already notice a difference in your demeanor. Just remember, stay positive through the process. Focus on each new opportunity as it crosses your path and pray to **GROW** through it."

"I will, Ezra, I will. You know what else, Ezra? I appreciate you sharing all of this. I'm glad I took a chance and spoke to you."

"So am I, Percy. I guess you had some confidence inside all along," I told him with a wink.

CHAPTER 9: HAVE FAITH

"*Three for three. Not bad, Teacher!*"

Thanks, Anabeth. The first three had gone well, but as I said earlier, I purposely started with the challenges and lessons I felt more comfortable dealing with to build momentum. Believe me, I needed some for the next one. Not only was I going to tackle one of the bigger challenges in the elevator, but I was also going to work with two people at once.

"*Eva and Adam!*"

Correct, Anabeth.

"*I was very curious about what was going on with those two when you introduced them.*"

Me too, Anabeth. When I placed my hands on them earlier, I felt a strong rush of emotions from deep within each. Sadness, despair, hopelessness, uncertainty, and love. What concerned me was that they seemed to emanate love so strongly as a couple, but individually, the love was being drowned by all those other emotions. I knew they needed my help and that I would do everything I could for them.

They were cuddled up together in the opposite corner of the elevator but still awake, so I made my way to that end without stepping on anyone and sat down facing them both. "How are you two holding up?" I asked.

As expected, Adam responded first. "Just great, Ezra. Thank you."

I was not particularly convinced, so I directed my attention to Eva. "I'll bet Adam would give me that answer no matter how he felt," I said with a slight smirk.

"You're right, he would. That's pretty much his standard," Eva replied with a grin as she gave Adam's knee a little squeeze.

"I figured. Don't worry, Adam. I stay very positive all the time myself. It helps in many situations like this one." I patted him on the back like an old pal.

"Exactly! See?" He pointedly asked Eva, then continued. "That's why I do it. I try to keep it positive for others. I know Eva doesn't like it all the time, but it's who I am."

Eva gave an unconvincing smile in return—the nonverbal equivalent of *Yes, honey. You're right.*

"Eva," I began, all my attention now on her. "Are you as positive as Adam?"

She looked at Adam, then back at me, and then back at him before she responded. "I try to be positive, but it doesn't come as easily for me. I've had a lot of negativity in my life, so it's definitely something I need to work on."

I did my best to affirm what she was saying. "Trying to avoid negativity is something we all need to work on, Eva. It must be difficult for you at times, though. I mean, constantly being around Mr. Positive over here?" I harmlessly nudged Adam and laughed to ensure my comment was received with levity.

Eva took the bait. "I never thought of it that way, but you're right. It does make it more difficult … a lot of the time."

Eva's words clearly stung Adam. He withdrew from their embrace and adjusted his sitting position, now leaning away from her. Still, he tried to brush it off. "Guess it's good we balance each other out. You know what they say, opposites attract, and all. Isn't that right, Eva?"

"Yes honey, that's right. We do balance each other out most of the time," she responded in a less-than-enthusiastic tone.

Adam looked marginally uncomfortable, both with the situation and with me. I needed to reestablish my connection with him before I could proceed. "You're a very lucky man, Adam, to have found your ideal match," I commented.

"Yes, I am!" he said with confidence.

"If only the rest of us could be so lucky," I added with a sigh, hoping Adam would follow my path of deflection.

"What about you, Ezra?" he asked. "Any significant other?"

It worked. "No, not yet, Adam. I have a lot of work to do on myself before I take on the responsibility of caring for another."

Adam bobbed his head in agreement. "I see it the same way! Taking care of another person is a big responsibility." Adam's subtext was clear to Eva, who was now the one stung. Her body language showed she had taken that comment right in the gut.

I quickly moved in to reestablish common ground. "Oh, it's definitely a big responsibility for *both* individuals to take care of one other. It's not one-sided, Adam." I smiled and gave Eva a nod to put some salve on the sting of Adam's remark.

Adam glanced at us, obviously realizing that his best option at that point was to agree and surrender. "Yes, that's what I meant too. It's our responsibility to take care of one another." Once again, he took Eva's hand.

I nodded in acceptance as I watched Adam and Eva lean against each other like pillars of support, united once again.

I had built some rapport and was gaining trust, so I took things up a notch. "Earlier, I promised to pray for you both when you told me that you had received some bad news today."

Both their heads dropped immediately, but then Eva's quickly raised like the sunrise, and she met my gaze with a clear sense of empowerment. "That's right, Ezra. We did receive some bad news from our doctor upstairs."

"Honey," Adam said quickly, "I thought you didn't want to discuss that with anyone. I thought—"

Eva cut him off. "It's okay, Adam. I'm ready to share our story. Besides, Ezra said he would pray for us, so he needs to know what to pray for. Right, Ezra?"

"Yes, I do prefer it that way. I think it makes it a little easier for God to answer our prayers when we're real specific." I smiled warmly.

Eva adjusted position, sitting up a bit taller. She wiped a couple tears that had left a glistening sheen on her cheeks and firmly clasped both of Adam's hands before beginning. "For as long as I can remember, I've wanted to be a mama. When I was just a baby myself, I would play with my dolls by feeding them, dressing them in cute little outfits, and changing their diapers. I would put them in tiny strollers and take them on walks, bathe them, and do all the things a real mother does for her babies. As I grew up, I continued to seek out children wherever I could. I didn't have any siblings, since I was adopted, so I played with my friend's younger siblings. I babysat as a teenager. I volunteered at the maternity ward as a candy striper and eventually chose a career where I would work with children on a daily basis."

"Yes, special needs children. That's really great," I said to show her I had been listening earlier.

She smiled, appreciating my supportive comment, but her eyes showed a deep sadness. "All the while, I figured I was preparing myself for motherhood. I was gaining the experience needed to be the best mama I could possibly be when my time arrived."

I continued to nod to show she had my full attention.

"When I met Adam, I was thrilled to learn that not only was he a wonderful man, but he also shared my love of children."

"Yes, I do, honey!" Adam made sure to proclaim.

Eva continued, "I can remember Adam and I having intimate conversations about parenting even back when we were in the early days of dating. We talked about everything, from preparing the nursery, to what sports our kids would play, to what schools they would attend. Even college. It was silly, but we enjoyed it." She giggled as she gazed off into the distance, immersing herself and us right along with her in those memories. "We were young but got married right after we finished grad school because we just couldn't wait any longer. We wanted to start a family as soon as possible."

"That's definitely a noble thing to want," I added, showing support for her beliefs.

"It may be noble, Ezra, but not always possible, unfortunately," Eva said sullenly as tears once again began to wet her cheeks.

Adam squeezed her hand. "You don't have to continue," he said quietly. "Would you like me to finish the story?"

Eva was quick to respond. "No honey, I've been holding this in for so long. It's good for me to get it all out."

I simply smiled in encouragement and waited.

"The first year or so wasn't bad. We had a lot of fun being newlyweds, along with the 'fun' that's a part of trying to get pregnant."

"Honey!" Adam blushed a little, which made her blush too. It was a cute "couple" moment. I reinforced the playful mood by putting my hand over my mouth like a child watching his parents kiss.

Eva and Adam were both surprisingly comfortable, which kept us headed in the right direction.

"Our first miscarriage came at about the two-year mark," Eva continued, "but it was very early on in the pregnancy, so we figured it wasn't meant to be. They are fairly common, according to our doctor. We didn't dwell on it too long and just kept trying. It was after the third miscarriage around year four that things started getting rough. That one came at twenty weeks, which was just long enough for us to get excited. At that point, we had prepared the nursery the way we had always wanted. We had a name picked out. We really thought it was going to happen ... before the massive disappointment came." Eva paused to stare off into the distance once again, although this time her thoughts seemed to drift away into more of a dark place than a dreamy memory.

Adam's urge to support his wife was great. He made an attempt to take over the story. "After the second miscarriage, the doctor said we needed to consider other options if we wanted to get pregnant."

"Other options?" I prompted.

"IVF. You know, In Vitro Fertilization. He told us that was our best option if we were to have any chance of getting pregnant. We looked into it and decided to give it a try."

"Hold on a minute, Adam," Eva interrupted. "It was not that simple. There's a lot more to the story than that." Eva looked at me, her eyes and frown heavy from carrying the weight of such heavy baggage. "What Adam is failing to mention is that it took another two years before we were even able to try IVF. It was two years of research and planning and saving money to be able to afford the procedure. It's very expensive, and our insurance didn't cover it. We got a little help from our parents, but they are all on fixed incomes, so most of the burden fell on us."

"I'm sure that was a very difficult time for both of you," I acknowledged.

"Yes, it was extremely difficult," Eva confirmed. "We were not our usual selves and fought more than we ever had before or have since. Still, we managed to make it through together."

"That's right, honey, and we're still together." Adam leaned in to give Eva a peck on the cheek.

Have Faith

"That's a testament to your marriage. I commend you both for your perseverance through all of that," I emphasized, wanting to highlight their strength through such adversity.

"Thank you, Ezra," they replied almost in unison.

Eva went on, "The first round of IVF didn't have the outcome we wanted. We ended up going through a couple more rounds over the next several years, all unsuccessful. All of that led us to our visit to the doctor's office here. We scheduled this appointment a few months back to plan for another round. We waited the required amount of time and had saved enough to try again." She paused one last time and wiped her face. I knew Eva was coming to the end of her story—and it was not the happy ending she had always wanted.

I offered support as best as I could, trying to lighten her burden. "That was the bad new news you mentioned earlier?" I questioned softly, knowing the answer.

"Yes. The doctor told us that there are no more options. My body can't take another round of in vitro treatment safely, so we have to give up. That's it. It's over. Time to accept that I will never be the mama I've always dreamed of." Eva's words trailed off as she broke down. Adam comforted her the only way he could, holding her as she placed her head on his chest and sobbed openly.

My immediate response was to say a quick prayer for them, while also praying that I would find the right words to console them.

"It's pretty sad, what they had to go through."

Yes, Anabeth, it is. That's why I also prayed that I could

provide some comfort to get them where they needed to be. Eva was doing her best to contain her emotions as she wept for her situation. I offered some support in the best way I knew how.

"I won't pretend to imagine what you are feeling right now or what it's like to go through everything you have gone through," I began consolingly. "What I do know for certain is that you are an incredibly strong woman, Eva. To have made it through all of that says a lot about your fortitude and character. Heck, just being able to share your story with me today shows your level of strength and perseverance."

Eva's tears had slowed, and she wiped her face again before sitting up to respond, "Thank you, Ezra. Most people don't see it that way. They always say Adam is the strong one and he holds me up. I think it's because he is always so positive, no matter what is going on, that sometimes it feels like it diminishes what I'm dealing with."

"What do you mean, Eva?" Adam probed with uncertainty.

"Honey, please don't take that the wrong way. You are definitely strong in your own right and you have been my rock of support through all of this. We couldn't have gotten through everything without each other. Still, it's my body, and I'm the one preventing us from having a baby. In the end, it's my fault."

Adam took back Eva's hands and held them close to his heart. "Oh, honey, it's not anyone's fault. We tried everything. It just isn't meant to be for us."

Eva nodded slowly, seemingly accepting their fate.

They had reached a low point; it was time for me to take action. "I disagree," I declared with the certainty of an expert authority on the witness stand. They both looked at me as if I had just transformed into an alien with tentacles popping out of my head. "I'm sorry, I disagree," I said again. "I don't believe that it isn't meant to be for you. In fact, I believe quite the opposite. I believe you are fated to be the mother you have always wanted to be, Eva. I also believe Adam will continue to be a very supporting husband and wonderful father."

They both sat staring at me in astonishment, yet I didn't budge or say another word.

Adam was the first to speak. "How can you say that?" he whispered. "How can you be so sure?"

"I am sure because you still have other options," I replied confidently.

Eva was now cautiously intrigued. "What are you talking about, Ezra? What have we not tried? What do you know that we don't?"

"God!"

They seemed surprised by my emphatic response.

"God. That's what I know. I know that God wants you to be the best mother that you can possibly be. You just need to try things a different way ... His way."

Eva's eyes gleamed with a new spark of excitement, while Adam's took on a glint of fury. He abruptly stood. "Look, Ezra, I can appreciate you being a religious guy and all, but we can't get our hopes up again after everything we've been through. That's just not fair to Eva."

Eva tugged on Adam's hand to bring him back down to ground level. "Hold on, Adam. Let's not discount what Ezra is saying. Please sit down." She turned my way. "Ezra, please continue."

"Look, I'm not some quack, nor am I some kind of miracle worker, but I do know scripture. Scripture tells us that when things seem hopeless and we are ready to quit, we need to do one thing: **HAVE FAITH** by trusting in God. There are many passages that speak to your situation. One stands out, based on everything you have told me: **Isaiah 66:9 'I will not cause pain without allowing something new to be born, says the Lord.'"**

Eva seemed a little dejected, as if she had been expecting me to reach behind my back at some point and produce a miracle baby for her. "But, Ezra, I have had faith throughout most of my struggles, and we still don't have a baby."

"Is that so?" I asked. "Where have you put your faith, Eva? In Adam? In the procedures? In the doctors? None of these places can answer your prayers. I seem to remember Adam saying earlier that both of you used to pray a lot more than you do nowadays. So, tell me, what changed? When did you stop praying? When did you lose faith in God?"

Eva gasped and burst into tears.

"That's enough!" Adam yelled, waking several others in the elevator. "You made your point, Ezra."

"But, but … ," I murmured, a little flustered.

"You can leave us alone now!" he insisted.

I instantly felt dejected. I had gotten caught up in the moment and pushed too hard. Surely, I had failed to help Eva and jeopardized helping the others.

"I didn't see that coming."

Yes, Anabeth, neither did I.

Sadly, I stood up and retreated to a neutral corner, then closed my eyes and began to pray for forgiveness. I started to doubt myself and why I was there. I tried to think clearly about helping the others but couldn't get my mind off of what had happened. It was very frustrating, so I just concentrated on my breathing and slowed everything down to hear God's voice in my heart. It took a few moments to get going, but then His voice came ... loud and clear. I began to hear words in my head. Over and over again: **HAVE FAITH, HAVE FAITH, HAVE FAITH.** It hit me like a heavyweight punch to the head. *Duh!* Here I was trying to teach them this exact lesson, and I wasn't even following my own advice. I had given up too soon. What a fool I was. Time to jump back in the ring, no matter the consequences.

I stood up and headed over to Eva and Adam, sitting down in front of them. Eva had stopped crying and Adam's facial expression indicated he was in a much calmer state.

"I'm very, very sorry. I don't mean any harm. Sometimes I get very passionate about God and my beliefs," I said with the sincerity of a sweet grandmother.

Eva clasped my right hand in both of hers. "It's okay, Ezra. I realize you were just speaking the truth ... and sometimes the truth is the hardest thing to hear. You're right. I did give up on God a long time ago when I didn't have a baby right away. I felt abandoned by Him, so I put my faith in everything but God. I can see now that the more I put my faith elsewhere, the more it took me away from God and the comfort only He provides. I feel so stupid. I was raised better than that. I don't know how I drifted so far."

"Don't beat yourself up, Eva. It happens to all of us sometimes." I placed a hand on my chest for emphasis. "A large part of Having Faith is learning to grow in your faith through different circumstances. You can consider the past few years of your life as a time of growth."

"That makes sense, Ezra." Eva nodded, then looked toward Adam. "I'm sorry if I wrongly put a lot of pressure on you, honey."

Adam cut her off before she could continue. "No, you've never put pressure on me. I'm your rock, remember. I'm here for you, and I always will be, Eva."

She pulled him in once again and gave him a quick kiss. Adam embraced her as long as Eva would let him, a warm, wide grin on his face. It was nice to see the comfort they offered each other, but I knew God could provide so much more for both of them.

I felt better now and sensed she was on track. "I have to say, Eva, I was a bit dejected a few minutes ago after I thought I had hurt you." She smiled warmly to reassure me she wasn't upset or offended, so I continued. "Now that you've acknowledged your feelings, I feel somewhat better but want to make sure you're comfortable with it all."

"Oh, I am, Ezra. It's funny, but when you challenged my faith it was like both a slap in the face and breath of fresh air at the same time. Like I said, I was raised in a faith-filled family. Growing up, we were always taught the importance of having faith in God and that He would always be there to help us in times of need. It's sad to realize that I drifted so far away so quickly and so easily."

"Sounds like a teaching moment to me!"

Yes, Anabeth, it was.

"I agree with you, Eva. It is sad—not about you, but about society in general. People all over the world, every day, make the same mistake you did. They know that they need to **HAVE FAITH** in God and that He is the Way, the Truth, and the Light, but they wrongly choose to put their faith elsewhere. In the end, such a choice usually leads to struggle, pain, or hopelessness, and then they come storming back wanting God to snap his fingers and fix their mess overnight."

"That's what happened with me," Eva said with obvious remorse.

"I know, Eva. Don't worry. The most important thing is that you are aware of the mistake you made and that you do something to change it."

"Oh, I am definitely going to change it! Now that I'm aware of it, I won't let it happen again."

I smiled. "How are you going to change, Eva?"

Eva paused, considering the question. She looked at Adam and again took his hands. "Honey, I'm done with all the doctors and the tests and procedures and the pressure we are putting on ourselves to have a baby. What do you say we stop all of it and just **HAVE FAITH** that God will lead us through our situation? What if we just believe that whatever happens will happen according to God's will and not ours?

What if we get back to living in peace and happiness, with no expectations like we did when we first got married? What do you say, honey?" Her voice cracked with emotion.

Adam took a long, slow deep breath as if he were inhaling her words and drawing them into his heart. "Are you sure, Eva? Is this what you really want?"

"Yes, honey, it is, with all my heart, but more importantly I want to know if it is what you want too."

Adam closed his eyes and lowered his head as if he were asking God to help him decide. He opened them after a moment with a warm smile. "Yes, Eva, I want all of that too. We can commit to God's plan instead of ours. Yeah, I like the sound of that. Less planning and organizing for me. I can get used to that," he said with a chuckle, and Eva and I soon joined in on the laughter.

"Don't worry, Adam. I'm sure God won't take all the planning and organizing off your hands! Just make sure that whatever you're doing, no matter who planned it, you **HAVE FAITH.**"

Adam and Eva looked at each other as if telepathically planning a joke, then they shouted out a resounding *"Amen!"*— as if trying to mimic mine from earlier. We all laughed as Adam even attempted to impersonate my deep voice—rather unsuccessfully.

"I bet that was pretty funny!"

Yes, Anabeth, it was!

When we had finished laughing and exchanging hugs of thanks, Eva decided to try and get some rest. She wedged her tired body between the wall and Adam's shoulder as best as she could and settled in. Adam and I talked for a few more minutes about how wonderful Eva was, faith-filled prayer, and how they would get back to attending church on Sundays. I could feel the honesty in his words as if they were coming straight from his heart. They sounded familiar and comfortable, like a child's favorite bedtime story repeated over and over without ever getting old. I took comfort knowing they were now on a solid path and would take whatever direction their faith in God led them.

CHAPTER 10: PRACTICE STILLNESS

"*You were right, Teacher. That was a tough one.*"

I guess you could say that, Anabeth, but not for someone I know.

"*You sound like your younger, cocky self!*"

Not at all, Anabeth! I'm not talking about me. Remember, nothing is impossible for God.

"*Well in that case ... I love that saying! You definitely had God working for you so far.*"

Yes, I did, Anabeth. Lucky for me, He would continue to help everyone else in the elevator. As time went on, I realized I could feel God's presence more and more. He was clearly working through me to provide whatever was needed—and what I needed at that point was a nap. Hours had already passed, and I was tired from working through the challenges of the first five passengers, but I knew I couldn't stop. If I were to help all ten of my newfound friends, I would need to keep moving systematically from one to the next.

I looked around for someone to engage next. It was an easy choice to make. The only other person still awake at that hour was Joshua, who was playing a game on his phone. He had some earbuds in his ears and seemed pretty focused on what he was doing. I was able to get his attention by mouthing, "Whatcha playing?"

He quickly glanced up but kept his attention on his phone. "Fortnite. Do you play?"

I didn't even know what that was, but I tried to brush it off. "No, I'm not really much of a gamer."

His fingers danced across his screen. "You should try it. It's awesome. I play all the time," he said, eyes fixed on the game.

I watched him, accessing the situation. I needed to engage him in a conversation one way or another, so I figured I'd just keep asking questions until something sparked his interest. "Do you usually play late like this, or is that just due to our situation?"

He didn't skip a beat on the game, his hands still moving faster than his mouth could speak. "Oh, yeah. I can play for hours. Sometimes, if I'm in a good game, I can play all night."

"Really? Wow. Doesn't it get difficult to sleep?"

"Nah, I don't sleep much. Don't have time for it. I'm too busy."

"Wait, what? You can't be serious," I said, sounding very dubious.

"Sure am!" he replied convincingly.

"Now that sounds crazy!" I said loudly, hoping to distract him enough to stop playing for a few minutes.

He didn't budge.

"What about work?" I pressed. "Doesn't that get difficult?"

"Not really. Nothing that coffee and a few energy drinks can't fix."

"I bet you could go for one of these energy drinks right now," I said invitingly, half-implying that I had one in my hand.

It worked! Joshua finally looked up for just long enough to make eye contact. "What? You have one? Oh … you don't. Bummer, I thought you said you had a spare energy drink." He sounded like a junkie just denied a fix. "Oh, shoot! I was all the way on level ten, and I died. Sucks. Oh, well, have to start over."

I placed my hand over the top of his screen to prevent him from beginning again. He looked up, slightly annoyed, but then he smiled, as he could tell I was being playful.

"How about you take a break for a few minutes and keep me company?" I suggested.

"Okay, I can take a break for a minute, Ezra. What's up?"

I had gotten him to stop but knew I needed to come up with something interesting to keep his attention. "You mentioned earlier that you used to be a competitive swimmer. That sounds pretty interesting. Tell me more about it."

"Swimming was pretty cool, and I was really, really good at it, which didn't hurt." He grinned and shrugged slightly.

"When did you first start swimming?"

"A long time ago. For as long as I can remember, really. My dad loves to tell the story of teaching me how to swim by throwing me in the deep end of our pool when I was a baby. I think I was actually, like, not even a year old when it happened, but I guess it worked, 'cause I became pretty good at a young age. My dad put me in competitions when I was only three, and I actually won some." He gave a short and slightly forced laugh.

"Wow, sounds pretty intense," I said, a vision of a diaper-wearing baby swimming across an Olympic-size pool flashing through my mind.

"I guess you could say that. My dad was pretty strict when I was young. He really pushed hard in training. Always wanted me to be the best and was intense."

He seemed to be opening up a bit, so I took a shot. "That must have put a lot of pressure on you."

"Yeah. I mean, maybe. I don't really think about it much anymore."

I persisted, "Maybe you don't think about it now, but I bet it was really difficult at the time it was happening."

"Sure, Ezra. It was difficult, but not as difficult as level ten of Fortnite!" He winked as he pulled out his phone to begin playing again. His face fell. "Shit! My phone died! You don't have one of those portable chargers, do you?"

"No. Sorry, Joshua. I don't."

He rummaged through his bag for a minute and then gave up.

I couldn't tell whether Joshua was more upset over the dead phone or the fact that he was now stuck talking to me again. Either way, I was going to get him engaged and talking about himself. "Tell me more about swimming. What was your favorite part of it?"

"The races, for sure. Training was long and tedious with my Nazi father, but the races were a different story. Those days always flew by. I'm not sure if it was the constant races or that there were so many of them, but it's all kind of a blur when I really think about it. I mean, I have tons of trophies and medals from racing events I can't even hardly remember. Come to think of it, if it weren't for my mom recording every meet, I wouldn't even know what happened half the time."

"That's very interesting," I noted curiously. "Why do you think that is?"

"I don't know. I never really thought about it. Maybe it had something to do with the races being so quick. I'd train for hours and hours, day after day, week after week, and then the races would only last seconds. I'd bet that has something to do with it."

"Could be," I agreed, sounding unconvinced, which clearly made Joshua uncomfortable.

"You disagree? What do think, then, Ezra?" he asked brusquely, in a tone he may have used with his Nazi father.

"I think that your assessment of it now may be a little off because you have a different perspective, looking at it years later."

"A little off?" Joshua frowned. "In what way?"

"That's for you to figure out."

Joshua was clearly growing more irritated. "Okay, now you sound like my father telling me I have to solve my own problems. Just say what you mean, please."

I humbled my tone in order to seem a bit less intimidating. "I'm sorry, Joshua. That wasn't my intention. I simply mean that to assess how you felt back then, you need to put yourself back in young Joshua's shoes."

"Okay? So how do I do that?" he demanded.

"You have to immerse yourself in the moment. Think of a specific race—perhaps a big race or one that seems more memorable than the rest. What comes to mind?"

"Junior National Championship," Joshua said immediately, looking suddenly thoughtful.

"Good, Joshua. Now, what do you remember specifically? Set the stage. Tell me every detail you remember."

"Let's see. I was twelve years old and had just placed first in the 100-meter freestyle at the Northwest regional the month before."

"That's good. Now, close your eyes and put yourself in that moment."

"I was the number-two seed behind Billy Phelps, who had won the Southeast regional. Billy had beaten me the year before when I tanked at the end of the race, so I was determined to not let that happen again." His tone grew a little fierce with the memory.

"You're doing great, Joshua. Now tell me about the race."

"Let's see. I was in lane three, and Billy was in lane four. I remember standing on the starting blocks as they announced us and looking over at Billy. He looked arrogant and cocky as he waved to the crowd—as if he were at the Olympic games in a foreign country. The rest of us, me included, just held up a hand to acknowledge we were there like we did at every other race. Anyway, I got my feet set and adjusted my cap and goggles one last time, as I always did. I visualized the race quickly in my head, dug my feet into the pad, and got ready for the all-too-familiar sound of the starting buzzer. I knew I needed to get off the blocks quickly, so I anticipated the exact moment and flew toward the water as the buzzer blared. It was a clean start, and I was off beautifully. I focused only on my strokes, my breath, and nothing else. The first fifty meters were blazing-fast. I hit the turn and felt as if I were in first place. I swam fluid and precise like a porpoise chasing its prey as I came down the home stretch. I kicked hard to the end and stretched out for the wall at the finish. It was a great race, and then it was over just as quickly as it began.

"And … ?" I prompted, surprised he had stopped his high-energy story. "What else do you remember?"

"That's it," he deadpanned.

"That's it?" I asked incredulously. "Did you win?"

"Hell, yeah, I won!" he confirmed with a huge smile and a laugh. "Of course, I won, Ezra! I not only won that race, but I set a Junior State record in the 100-meter freestyle that still stands today."

"That's awesome, Joshua!" I congratulated with heartfelt enthusiasm.

He smiled cockily. "More importantly, I beat Billy by a full second. Someone said they heard him crying in the locker room afterward, but I never knew if that was true."

"Quite an accomplishment."

"Yep. It was, at the time. I know I was pretty excited after it was over and for the rest of the meet. Oh, yeah—my team even won the 4 x 100-meter freestyle relay, where I swam the anchor leg. I think we set a record for that too. Man, I had totally forgotten about the relay until now." His eyes drifted off as if he were still sifting through the thrills of those memories.

"Sounds like it was a great meet," I said, trying to encourage him further.

"Yes, it was. Our team did pretty well. We came in third or fourth, overall, I think."

"That's great, Joshua. So, what do you remember about the rest of the day? What type of feelings did you have afterward?"

"Feelings?" Joshua blinked and looked at me in confusion as if I had spoken in a foreign language.

"Yes, remembering how you felt will help you recall the rest of the details," I explained.

"Let's see. I know I was happy. I can tell you that."

"That's a start. Did anything besides the race affect your feelings that day?"

"Hunger. Yes, hunger. It was such a long meet that we left late and hit traffic. We were on the stupid bus forever before we stopped to eat. We did go to my favorite pizza place, so that was good. You know what? My father even gave me some money to play video games at the restaurant, which was rare."

"I bet you enjoyed that. What game did you play?"

"GTA, of course. That was my favorite back then. If you think I play Fortnite too much, you should have seen me back then. I played GTA, like, 24-7."

I didn't want to get back on the topic of video games, so I immediately refocused him. "See how that worked, Joshua? Do you understand how putting yourself in the moment and feeling the way you did back then helped you remember the details?"

"Yes, I get it, Ezra. My swimming coach had me do the same type of thing in practice. He called it slowing down in the moment."

I nodded and smiled. "That's one way to look at it, 'slowing down in the moment,' which I'm sure helped as you practiced your swimming. I believe I see a need for a different type of practice in your life now."

"Really? What type of practice do I need now?"

I had piqued his interest and needed to hammer home the point. "Stillness, Joshua. You need to **PRACTICE STILLNESS.**"

"**PRACTICE STILLNESS?** What does that mean?"

"It means that you need to take the time to meditate or pray and just be present with yourself. Everything you have been telling me about your life is go, go, go, and doing, doing, doing. There is no stillness in your life, and it is taking its toll on you."

Joshua was clearly caught off guard a bit and seemed a little perturbed. "Oh, come on! I know I do a lot, but I have time for myself."

"Really? When you're playing video games or looking at social media on your phone?"

"Yeah, I'm alone most of those times, so it's just me, myself, and I."

Joshua was not taking this as seriously as I had hoped, so I decided to be even more authoritative.

"I know what that's like."

Yes, you do, Anabeth. I needed him to know too.

"Okay. I can see you're trying to be humorous, but that's not what I mean," I said. "You need some time that is 100-percent distraction-free. Some time for your brain to 'unplug,' where there is no other stimulus around. No alerts, notifications, reminders, or—most importantly—people. Just you and your mind and heart. When you **PRACTICE STILLNESS**, it allows you to not only take true time for yourself but also to focus on those things that really matter in your life."

"But all of the things that you say, *go, go, go,* and *do, do, do,* are the things that matter to me."

"Yes, I know they matter, and they do have value to you in your life, Joshua. Is it possible that you are placing too much value on these types of things and not enough on yourself?" I knew the answer to this but needed him to acknowledge it. If he allowed himself to be vulnerable, he could open his heart.

He seemed to mull that over. "Yes, it's possible, I suppose."

The door had cracked open. It was time to get more real and direct. "Okay, that's a start. What is it about your life that you feel is not valuable, Joshua?"

He paused as if really thinking about it, and I sensed his vulnerability increasing. "I don't know. I never thought about that … I mean, about my life not having value. I just figured by focusing on others, I would be better off."

"Yes, Joshua, it is noble to think about others and help them. Your service in Big Brother is an example of work that has great value for others."

Joshua nodded, seeming more at ease. "I think so."

"For sure, it does. By taking time to **PRACTICE**

STILLNESS, you can really reflect on work like this without distraction. This allows you to see the true value in what you do for others, yourself, and even the world. It allows you to receive the joy, happiness, and fulfillment you have been missing. It can effectively change this work from mere activities to transformations for you and others."

"Transformations?" He shook his head, puzzled. "What do you mean by that?"

"I mean that you can be transformed into the person that you were meant to be. The best version of yourself. Not just someone who goes through the motions, but someone who is truly living and making a difference."

His mouth formed a thin line. "Goes through the motions, huh? Is that what you think about my life? My father used to say almost the exact same thing whenever he thought I wasn't putting in 100-percent effort in the pool."

"Look, Joshua, you don't need to listen to me, your father, or anyone else. You just need to listen to yourself. That's what I meant when I told you to **PRACTICE STILLNESS**. By Practicing Stillness, you can actually hear the voice inside that will point you in the right direction. That voice will lead you in your transformation."

I couldn't tell if I was having an impact or if he was just getting annoyed with me, but he was unquestionably listening as he sat like a kindergartener waiting for the teacher to finish the story, his elbows planted on his crossed legs with his hands resting on his chin.

After a few seconds of silence, he said, "I can see that you are not like my father, Ezra. You're different. You seem to understand what's going on with me, even though we only met a couple hours ago. It's a little weird but cool at the same time. I'm getting what you're saying but want to know more about this transformation part you just mentioned."

Bingo. He was listening. "A transformation is basically a thorough or dramatic change. Think caterpillar to butterfly."

"Makes sense for a butterfly." He chuckled a little. "But what about me?"

"I'm not going to answer that question. You're going to answer it yourself," I responded before he could object.

He held up a hand. "Wait, uh—"

"Nope, not yet! First, close your eyes and take a minute to **PRACTICE STILLNESS** before you answer. Just focus on your breath to start. Breathe slowly for four seconds in and four seconds out. This will help to clear your mind from all the distractions around you. After that, you can think about the caterpillar and butterfly. How would each one feel? What does the transformation look like? These questions will help you understand the path I am showing you."

He gave me a dubious look. "Okay," he finally agreed. "Here goes nothing."

Joshua did as instructed, closing his eyes and taking long, slow breaths. His body was still; he appeared dialed in. He sat there for three to four minutes until a hint of a smile appeared on his face, and I saw his eyes open. "I get it … I mean, I have an answer, Ezra!"

"That's great, Joshua," I said with delight.

Joshua continued excitedly, "Right now, I am living my life like a caterpillar. I am crawling around on the ground like a worm, not having an impact on anyone but myself. If I can transform to the best version of myself, then I will be like the butterfly, taking to the sky and flying high as a beautiful creation, sharing my beauty and positively impacting others around me."

I smiled widely, showing my immense pride. "I couldn't have said it better myself, Joshua. You not only got your answer, but you also practiced stillness beautifully. How did it feel?"

He mulled over the question. "Surprisingly good, actually. I didn't think I would like the whole stillness thing. It's not what I'm used to, but the breathing really helped me zone in. It reminded me of swimming with my head under the water, where there are no other sounds but my own thoughts. It was cool. I could do it again."

"That's wonderful, Joshua! I'm very proud of the way you picked it up so fast and put it to good use."

He beamed. "Yeah, I'm naturally good at most things," he said, half-joking, but also half-serious as he brushed his fingernails across his chest.

"Okay, okay, Mr. Natural. If you really want to see an impact, then make it a regular part of your life," I instructed.

"How?" he asked with true sincerity.

"Begin to **PRACTICE STILLNESS** daily for five to ten minutes, or better yet, twice a day. I've found that the best times to do this exercise are first thing in the morning and right before bed. You'll see some real magic if you **PRACTICE**

STILLNESS before you do anything else for the day, especially before picking up your phone." I winked at him.

"That may be difficult," he said, almost gritting his teeth at the thought. "But I'll give it a try."

"How about this: You like to work out, correct?"

"Yeah."

"Have you ever done one of those challenges at the gym where you do something every day for sixty days without fail?" I asked.

He waved his hand. "Sure. I've done lots of them. They're always easy for me 'cause of all the swimming discipline I put in over the years."

"Perfect! Just consider this exercise as one of those challenges. **PRACTICE STILLNESS** for the next sixty days first thing in the morning and before you go to bed. I guarantee you'll see even better results than you did with any of those physical challenges, Mr. Natural."

Joshua scoffed and then laughed at my lighthearted teasing. "All right. I'll do it. I will **PRACTICE STILLNESS** for the next sixty days and see what kind of impact it has." He extended his hand to shake mine. "Deal."

"Deal, Joshua." I pumped his arm a few times. "But you have to promise to let me know how it impacts you."

"You got it!" Joshua released my hand and put his earbuds back in his ears. I knew his phone was dead but took it as a sign that he wanted some alone time, so I stood up to stretch for a minute.

"Teacher, I like how you helped him to see the value of Practicing Stillness, but something is missing."

Missing? What's that, Anabeth?

"God! You didn't add in the importance of God being a part of his stillness, or even prayer, for that matter."

That's correct, Anabeth. Not yet, I didn't. Working with Joshua proved more difficult than I originally thought. Yes, he was beginning to understand transformation, and yes, we were able to channel his competitive nature to **PRACTICE STILLNESS,** but he still had a long way to go. He was not ready for that yet. Don't forget, as I spoke with him, I was constantly praying to do God's will. I knew that things would move at the pace of God's time, so I didn't rush anything. Remember, there were still many more souls to help in that elevator.

"Thank you. Now I understand, Teacher. So, who did you help next?"

CHAPTER 11: LOVE

Tell me, Anabeth, who would you have helped next?

"Let's see … So far, you've taught Carly to Show Gratitude, Matt to Be Present, Percy to Grow, Eva and Adam to Have Faith, and Joshua to Practice Stillness. Those are some good lessons, but you haven't even gotten to the big ones yet."

Which lessons are you referring to, Anabeth?

"You know, the ones that God and all the Angels have abided by since the beginning of time: to Love, Give, and Serve one another."

That's correct, Anabeth. I hadn't gotten to the big three yet. Which one would you go with next?

"Love. Definitely Love."

So sure of yourself, are you? And why would you go with Love next?

"That's easy. Because Love is the most important of the three. It's the foundation to build everything else upon."

That's very good, Anabeth, and very true. I did choose Love as the next lesson. So, who do you think I taught the lesson to?

"Let's see. Who's left … ? You still have Faith, John, Betty, and Olivia, right?"

That's correct.

"Out of those four, I think two of them align better with Giving and Serving, so that leaves either Faith or Betty."

Pretty good deductive reasoning, Anabeth. You must have a good teacher.

"Yeah, he's okay, I guess."

Ha-ha, very funny. You better be respectful if you want to hear the rest of the story, kiddo.

"Sorry, Teacher! You know I'm a jokester like you used to be!"

True. So, who would you pick?

"That's a tough one. They both could use a lesson on Love."

Once again, you're correct, Anabeth. However, one of them couldn't have a lesson on Love until she had another lesson first. All right, you have a fifty-fifty shot at getting it right. Who's it gonna be?

"Faith. I'm going to say Faith."

Sorry, Anabeth. Betty was the one I chose. You are right in saying that Faith needed to learn about Love as well, but it was crucial she be taught a different lesson first.

"What else did Faith need to know, then? You have to tell me now!"

More on that later. You'll understand when we get there.

"Aww, man!"

Don't worry. I promise it will all make sense in God's time.

So, as you said, Betty was ripe for a lesson on Love. Not only was her heart screaming for it, but I had picked up on things from her words and actions earlier that pointed toward Love. She had lived a long life and had a big family, but something was missing. There was a gap between her heart and her mind that wasn't allowing Love to flow as it should. I prayed that I would be able to help her in the way she needed as I waited patiently for an opportunity to speak with her. She had been napping on and off for the past couple of hours, so I knew it was only a matter of time before she woke up.

Lucky for me, I didn't have to wait long. A short time later she started to get a bit restless before opening her purse to dig for buried treasure once again. I saw this as the opportunity I needed to engage her in conversation. I moved closer and knelt down on one knee beside her. "Can I help you with anything, Betty?"

She looked up a little foggily as if she didn't remember who I was for a moment, before she said, "Oh. Hi, Ezra. I don't need any help, but maybe I can help you."

"Help me?" I repeated, intrigued.

"Yes, like I did last time with the water," she reminded me.

"Yes, yes, thank you. The water was very helpful when I needed it. What are you in need of?" I asked.

"A snack. It's after midnight, and I forgot to take my heart medication with all the commotion. So, I need to take it now. If I don't take it with food, I get an upset stomach, and that I don't need right now, considering everything else going on."

"Oh, I see." I nodded. "That's important. Do you have some food in your bag?"

She glared at me. "Obviously, or I wouldn't be looking in my purse."

I sought to make her more comfortable—or at least ask less of a dumb question. "Sorry. I meant, do you have enough snacks in there to share with me?"

Her demeanor instantly changed from irritated to fostering, which confirmed my earlier assessment of her emotional state. "Of course, Ezra! Let's find you something to eat." She resumed her search and pulled out a granola bar and a bag of peanuts. "Does one of these work?"

"Yes, definitely. Which one do you need to take with your medication? I will take the other."

"You don't worry about me. Just take the one you like best." She held out both options.

I glanced at the food and then at her. "Are you sure?"

"Of course!"

"Okay. I'll take the granola bar." I held out my hand and she eagerly put the bar in it. "Thank you, Betty."

"You're welcome, Ezra. Now eat up. You're a growing boy, so you need it."

I took a bite and produced a look of enjoyment, despite not having any concept of the flavor.

"How weird. You ate it! What did it taste like?"

It's too difficult to explain right now, Anabeth. Besides, it's not really relevant.

I continued to eat the bar as Betty opened the bag of peanuts for herself. "I always have snacks on hand," she informed me. "Learned that with my grandson, Charlie. He's probably about your age and can eat like a horse."

Bingo! She had revealed what would get us talking about Love, so I broached the subject. "That's right, Betty. You mentioned that you have twenty-two grandchildren, whom you Love very much."

She nodded. "Glad you were paying attention, Ezra. I don't know if everyone else in here was as interested in my story as you."

I looked at her with disbelief. "Really? I enjoyed hearing about your family and your birthday."

"Thank you," she said with satisfaction.

"Do you have any pictures of your family you can show me?" I questioned with interest.

"Pictures? Oh, do I? Yes … yes! I have lots of pictures! Let me just find my phone." She dug through a bag within her purse until she pulled out a small leather pouch, which encased her phone. "I know there are a lot of pictures on Facebook. My daughters post them all the time so I can keep up. Let me just pull it up … Darn it. It's not working for some reason."

Betty stood up and held her phone as high as she could while waving it back and forth frantically. "This lousy phone won't work."

Betty's actions caught the attention of the only other person even remotely awake, Faith, who offered some advice. "Sorry, Betty, there's no coverage in the elevator. We all tried for a long time when we first got stuck."

Betty looked down with irritation at Faith, who was sitting in the corner, and said, "Yes, young lady, I may be old, but I remember what happened earlier. I just wanted to see if anything had changed by now."

Faith's sleepy eyes closed as she mumbled, "Sorry, just trying to help."

"*Excuse me?*" Betty snapped.

Faith timidly muttered, "I was just saying good luck. Hope it works for you," and then closed her eyes to prevent any further engagement.

Betty rolled her eyes at Faith and then fixed her attention back on me. "Sorry, Ezra, I'll have to show you the current pictures later. I have a few old ones in my wallet, though." After another extensive purse search, she drew out a large woman's wallet with an accordion picture holder tucked inside. It held about twenty pictures that had clearly tucked into those tiny plastic folders for years. The corners were missing on most of them, and the edges were frayed. Luckily, I could make out the picture in the middle of each 2x3 window. Betty held them up for me to see but strangely would not let go of the wallet when I attempted to take it for a closer look. She began to launch into detailed descriptions of each. "This is a picture of me and my children back when we were a younger family altogether. This is obviously me. Then, you have my daughters, Mary, Lizzie, Linda, and Lori. Then, my sons, Anthony, and Albert, and Zach." She had pointed to everyone in the picture but left out the man who was unquestionably her husband.

"This must be your husband," I remarked innocently, pointing to his face. "What's his name?"

She sighed out coldly, "Ex-husband. His name is Joseph." It was evident she had left him out intentionally, for reasons known only to her.

It wasn't my place to ask yet, so I simply said, "That's a good-looking bunch. I can definitely see the family resemblance."

Her scowl immediately transformed into a sunny smile. "Yes, they are. You may not know it now, but I was quite the looker when I was younger, Ezra."

I think I blushed a little as I said, "I'm sure you were Betty, and still are." I nudged her arm with a smile and gave her a wink.

She giggled, smiled back, and then returned to her pictures. "Here are some of my grandbabies. They're mostly older now, but they'll always be babies to me." She shared various school and sports pictures of her grandchildren as she thumbed from one to the next. With each picture, she beamed with the joy of a mother in the maternity ward.

I could feel her Love emanating strongest at this point, so I immediately put my focus there. "I can tell you Love them all very much, Betty."

"Absolutely! they're my pride and joy, Ezra."

"I'm sure they are," I said affirming her role as the matriarch. "Thank you for sharing the pictures with me, Betty. I really enjoyed them."

She looked at me as if I were a used car salesman selling a lemon. "Seriously, Ezra? You enjoyed that? Most young people don't have time for us old folks anymore."

I placed my hand on her shoulder to show my sincerity. "That's not how I was raised, Betty. I was taught to always have time for everyone, especially those in need."

She gave me a funny smile and retorted, "That's nice, but I'm not really in need."

"Oh, I know, Betty, not in that sense. I just remember that earlier, when you mentioned your grandchildren, you started to get a little emotional. I just wanted to offer some comfort."

Annoyance abruptly clouded her features. "I told you all that I wasn't crying. It was just my allergies from this stuffy elevator and that big man's cologne." She threw a dirty look at Big John, who was resting and had no knowledge that he was now the target of Betty's angst.

I smiled softly. "You're right. This elevator *is* stuffy, and Big John's cologne is kind of strong."

She smiled with the satisfaction of someone being told they were right. I continued with my hand once again on her shoulder. "Still, I can't help but feel that talking about your family made you a little choked up and sad."

Betty hesitated for a moment. "I just get sad because I miss my grandbabies," she finally said, her voice cracking. "I don't get to see them very often lately. They're growing up so fast and don't have time for me much anymore. I call and even text them, 'cause they never want to talk on the phone, but they still don't reply." She gave a little shrug, her voice growing stern again. "They have their own lives and I have mine, so it's fine." She pulled a tissue out to blow her nose. "See? I told you, allergies."

Betty was still holding on to her stoic facade. Clearly, she responded best when allowed to maintain a sense of control. She would need to be comfortable with my forward and direct questions before she would open up. "Betty, I'm sure your grandkids Love and miss you a lot too. I bet you spoil them when they're with you."

Betty giggled like a mischievous child. "Well, maybe just

a little. I know all their favorite candies and snacks, so I have them on hand whenever I see them. Their parents complain later, but I don't care. That's what grandmas are for. Plus, I let the kids help me with all the things they enjoy, like the computer."

"That sounds nice," I said warmly. "Do you get a lot of individual one-on-one time with them?"

"No, not since they were babies. Now, it's only during family events like birthday parties."

"It sounds like the time you get to spend with them is pretty busy," I commented.

"Yeah, it's never enough. I also always need to get back to my residence, which the kids never want to be a part of, and it takes away time from their other activities too, which they complain about." Betty's unhappiness over the situation was apparent.

I took the hint. "You know what, Betty? I bet you would really enjoy some one-on-one time with each grandchild."

"Of course I would! That's what I enjoyed the most when they were small. I would get to take care of each of them for extended periods of time, and we could really connect. I miss that a lot."

"Yes, connecting is very important with all the ones you Love. Did you connect the same way with your children when they were little?"

Betty once again hesitated before she responded. "No, it was different with my seven—that's what we used to call them, by the way. With my seven, Joseph and I never agreed on how to raise them, so I didn't have the same connection as I do with my grandbabies. Joseph and I were also at odds a lot, which made it difficult on my seven."

"That must have been difficult, even for you, Betty," I offered, wanting to show my concern yet build trust between us at the same time.

She jeered at me with a bit of uncertainty. "What do you mean, even for me?"

"Oh, I just mean that you are clearly a very strong woman, who is always able to handle things, aren't you?"

"Of course, I am, Ezra!" she agreed, straightening a little. "I *am* strong. I have always had the answers and still do today."

She responded exactly as I had expected and was heading right where she needed to go, even though she didn't yet know it. "Yep, I figured that was the case," I affirmed, backing up her comment and steering her toward agreement. "Those are good traits to have as the matriarch and leader of the family. In that role, you obviously know one of the strongest things you can do is realize when you don't have the answer and let yourself be vulnerable." I kept nodding during that last statement, hoping that would help gain her affirmation.

She sat still, soaking in what I had said. I had painted her into a corner. Now, she only had two options: either agree with me in order to maintain her aura of strength, or disagree, discrediting herself and showing she was not as strong as she thought.

Unfortunately for me, she chose an alternative option: deflection, which meant she was trying to retreat. "What time is it, Ezra? I need to take my medication."

"It's 12:30 a.m., Betty. You already took your medication when we had our snacks a little while ago."

"Oh, that's right. No wonder I'm getting a little tired."

I wasn't going to let her off so easily. She was suffering and needed my help. "I'm very sorry to hear that, Betty. I was really enjoying hearing about your family, and you were teaching me a lot. I'd Love to continue chatting for just a few more minutes, unless, of course, you're too tired ...."

Betty straightened up as a show of strength. "No, no. I'm not too tired. We can keep talking. You're an okay listener, so why not? What were we talking about again?"

Bingo. I disregarded the half-compliment and sought to bring her home. "You were just telling me how sometimes as the matriarch you have to let yourself be vulnerable to the ones you **LOVE** when you don't have an answer. Sometimes you have to let **LOVE** come first before your strength or pride. You were saying that **LOVE** is the most important part of family and of life."

She gave me the kind of surprised look of someone given too much change at the grocery store after the cashier had assured them they had paid twenty dollars when they knew they only paid with a ten-dollar bill. "Yes, that's right. That's what I was saying, Ezra. I always say that **LOVE** is the most important thing. Guess you're a good listener, after all."

"Thank you, Betty. I agree with you 100 percent. **LOVE** is the most important part of any relationship, especially within a family. When there is **LOVE** in a relationship, there is a solid foundation to build everything else." Betty was nodding away, so I just kept going. "You mentioned your religious education and daily prayer, so I know you'll agree with me when I say, I believe every second we get to spend with the ones we **LOVE** is very precious and truly a gift from God." I continued the affirming body language to gain more agreement.

This time, I had given her only one avenue, which she took, aligning us further. "Most definitely, Ezra. I send my family prayers and special messages that say things like that all the time."

"Those types of prayers are nice," I said, keeping her moving where she needed to go. "What do your children and grandchildren think about them?"

"Who knows?" she grumbled with a shrug.

I frowned. "I'm sorry. What do you mean, Betty?"

"I mean that they never respond, so I don't know what they think."

Her answer was cold, so I knew something was missing. "How do they respond when you tell them these things in person?" I asked.

Betty was starting to fidget a bit.

I pressed on before she could answer or deflect again. "You know, how do they respond when you tell them how precious they are to you and how much you **LOVE** them?"

Betty sat stunned, staring off into the distance as if the elevator wall went on for miles. She had reached a point of realization in her heart and needed to acknowledge it but was letting her stoicism and stubbornness win the battle. I simply smiled and nodded, hoping she would answer. She continued to fidget and then started digging through her bag. Oh, no! She was trying to escape the uncomfortable question like she had before. I had led her down the path, gaining agreement with her along the way, yet she was still attempting to revert to her old ways.

We both sat silent and motionless for what seemed like an eternity, so I gave her a nudge. "Betty, you've told us all and especially me how much you **LOVE** your family. Your stories and descriptions of them have spoken of **LOVE** as well. It's obvious to me that you **LOVE** your family, and even though I don't know them personally, I'm sure they **LOVE** you too. I just have to ask one thing that I haven't heard you mention the whole time we've been in the elevator: How often do you tell individual family members that you **LOVE** them?"

Betty's demeanor didn't change much at first. She just kept staring at the wall. I was a little concerned that I had pushed too hard but stayed quiet this time and waited patiently. After about three minutes had passed I started getting worried. Was she just physically tired due to the lateness of the night? Was her blood sugar low? Oh, my goodness—had she just suffered a stroke? I needed to see if I had to intervene, so I reached out to pat her on the shoulder. She glanced toward me with a hint of a tear in the inside corner of her left eye. After another minute, she finally spoke. "I don't think I like your questions, Ezra. Why are you asking me such things? Are you trying to hurt me?"

Her words stung. My ears filled with fire and ice, ringing from her emotion. Betty had reached her breaking point. My final question had helped her realize that she was not truly showing her family **LOVE**, and this realization was hurting. She was more concerned with maintaining a façade of strength in her role of matriarch then that of a loving mother or grandmother. More concerned with being right rather than being loved. I instantly prayed that she would acknowledge the truth so she could move forward as I responded supportively with **LOVE**.

"Betty, I'm sorry. I do not mean to offend or hurt you in any way. I am only trying to live as an example of what God wants for each and every one of us. That's why I prayed the way I did for everyone in the elevator when we first got stuck. It was to take the experience as one of **LOVE** and grace.

"Betty, we both agree that **LOVE** is the most important part of all relationships. It's the foundation on which to build a strong family. I know how strong you are, and I want to help you use this strength to share your **LOVE** with others, especially your family."

Betty sat solemnly for just a few seconds this time before speaking up. "I guess you weren't trying to hurt me after all. You're an interesting young man, Ezra. I think I'm glad we are having this conversation."

It was a start, so I pressed on. "Betty, since we both agree on the importance of doing God's work, how would you answer my last question: How often do you tell your individual family members that you—?"

"You don't have to repeat the question. I heard you the first time. The answer is never, all right? I never actually tell them out loud because they should know by now. I've spent my whole life being a mother and grandmother, which I think is enough **LOVE** for one person. Everything that I've done for them says that I **LOVE** them."

"You're right, Betty," I said with a great deal of sincerity and empathy. She finally smiled, so I immediately continued with, "Being a mother and grandmother is one of the most important things in the world. It's also one of the most challenging."

"Amen to that!" Betty agreed enthusiastically.

"Yes, Betty. Amen to that." I grinned. "You've also had an immense impact on your children and grandchildren throughout the process, have you not?"

"Absolutely!" Betty was getting as fired up as an eighty-year-old grandma could.

"So, tell me, was it all worth it?"

"Of course, it was! No matter how many poop-filled diapers I changed or how much vomit I cleaned up, it was most definitely worth it." Betty, practically shouted, a lifetime of memories pouring out of that one sentence.

"Okay, so, if it is truly worth it, and you truly **LOVE** them, then it is necessary to remind them of this as often as you can. This will allow **LOVE** to be at the forefront of your relationships. It will make **LOVE** more important than being right or strong. **LOVE** will keep a solid family foundation so it lasts a lifetime. That's what I will pray for you and your family."

I closed my eyes immediately to discourage a response. Silently, I sat down on the floor to briefly pray and let my words sink in for both of us. When I opened my eyes, Betty was wiping away her tears.

"Were you really just praying for me and my family, or did you just say that to make me feel better?" she asked softly.

"Yes, Betty. I most certainly was praying for you. I prayed that you and your family will tell each other how much you **LOVE** them, that you will put **LOVE** first before all else, that **LOVE** will be at the forefront of your relationships, and that **LOVE** will be the biggest part of your lives from now on. God wants you to understand the importance of having **LOVE** in your life and the importance of sharing this gift because when you share **LOVE** with your family, you are sharing a gift from God."

Betty let out a long breath. "I have to tell you, Ezra, I'm an eighty-year-old woman who received religious education throughout my life. I know the Bible. I know what **LOVE** is."

I couldn't quite tell whether Betty was agreeing or disagreeing, so I aimed to reinforce the point. "I can see that you do, Betty, which is why I'm enjoying our conversation so much," I said to diffuse any aggression, then continued, "Then you also know the strength and power of **LOVE**. You know that the woman you are today is the result of God's **LOVE**. Without God's **LOVE**, you, your family ... all of it would be nothing."

"Yes, Ezra. I know all these things. I may not act like it all the time, but I know them."

She was beginning to let go, so I kept on positively reinforcing while chipping away at her armor of stubbornness. "I'm glad you acknowledged that, Betty. That shows that you want to have **LOVE** at the center of your life. It shows that God can work through you to better share **LOVE** with your family. It shows that with a little bit of change and God's help, you can gain deeper connections with the ones you **LOVE**."

Betty had been nodding with her eyes wide open as I was speaking. "I, I …." She was about to respond, probably to express a bit of her old stubbornness, when her mouth began to quiver. She could not hold it in any longer. She had reached a point of acceptance, in which she understood the importance of my words and the need for change in her life. She hung her head slowly as she began to cry, not with the tears of a broken-down woman but with those of a woman showing the strength to improve herself to support the ones she loved. Her sobs were both a release and a cry of joy, as if Betty was screaming from the rooftop. I could feel that this was a lot for her to handle at once, so I quickly moved in to show as much loving support as I could.

"You are so wonderfully strong, Betty! I bet God is smiling and very proud of you right now, and I'm sure your family would be beaming with **LOVE** if they were here."

Betty wiped her eyes and sat up a bit straighter. I waited patiently as she took out a small mirror to check her appearance. She made sure her makeup still looked presentable, then told me something that threw me for a loop. "You must be an Angel, Ezra."

Caught off guard, I almost said something revealing before she continued. "Only an Angel could get a stubborn old broad like me to realize I need more **LOVE** in my life."

I laughed to diffuse her comment, though I still trembled a bit inside at the thought of her unveiling my secret. Luckily, she continued on as her usual self, providing me a reprieve. "So, you're saying I need to tell my family I **LOVE** them more, is that it?"

"Yes," I agreed. "And that's just the start. I'm saying you need to let **LOVE** lead you all the time. Let it be the center of all your actions and interactions with others. By doing, so you will open the door to God's presence, which will make everything a million times better."

She nodded vehemently. "I want that. I don't know how many more years I have left on this rock, but I know that I'd better make sure I don't waste any more of them."

I smiled with subtle joy. Betty's eyes had been opened, and she was finally in a place of realization of her actions in life. I wanted to give her a way to facilitate change within herself, so I looked no further than some of my favorite scripture. "Betty, are you familiar with the scripture, **1 Corinthians 13:4-7?**"

"I believe so. It's about **LOVE** isn't it?"

"Yes, Betty. I'm sure you've heard it before. Let me share **1 Corinthians 13:4-7: 'Love is patient, love is kind. It does not envy, it does not boast, it is not proud. It does not dishonor others, it is not self-seeking, it is not easily angered, it keeps no record of wrongs. Love does not delight in evil but rejoices with the truth. It always protects, always trusts, always hopes, always perseveres.'"

"Oh, yes, of course. That was a reading at my daughter Lori's wedding. I really like that one."

"Great, Betty. This scripture provides perfect instructions for you to follow as you work toward improving your life through **LOVE**. Next time you are in a difficult situation with a family member, just think of the words from this passage, and you will know what to do."

"That's a good idea, Ezra." She smiled warmly. "I think they have that scripture on prayer cards at the church store. I'll pick one up and keep in in my purse."

"Sure, Betty, whatever you can do to make it easy," I said with a thumbs-up and returned her smile.

"Oh, it's not going to be easy, by any stretch of the imagination. Remember, I've built up a lot of habits in my eighty years of life, and I'm sure not all of them are good."

"That's okay. We all have habits, Betty. The important thing is to make them work to our advantage. How about if you make it a habit to read your prayer card with 1 Corinthians 13:4-7 every morning. This way, you will keep it fresh in your memory."

"Sure, if I can remember to read it," Betty responded quickly in her usual fashion.

I didn't want to let her stray too easily, so I summed things up in the best way I knew how. "I'm sure you will remember. I'll pray for that too."

"Thank you, Ezra. I may have said this already, but you're a very interesting young man. I've enjoyed speaking with you, but it's very late, and I'd really like to get some rest now." Her eyes were starting to droop, and her voice sounded heavy.

"Oh, yes, of course," I agreed hastily. "I loved our conversation. It was very special for me too. You're right once again, Betty. It is late. I think I'll get some rest too."

Betty reclined in an empty corner of the elevator and used her big purse as a makeshift pillow. I continued some final prayers of thanks to God for all that had just transpired. I also prayed for everything that I had promised Betty I would include. Most of all, I prayed that Betty would not forget what she had learned and that she would make **LOVE** the most important part of her life from here on out.

"Wow! That sounded exhausting."

What do you mean, Anabeth?

"It just sounded like it took so much work to get her to understand the importance of Love."

You can look at it that way, Anabeth. I, however, didn't see it as work, but as my duty to share what God wanted for Betty and all of his children. You see, Anabeth, it's not just the job of Angels to help humans understand how important Love is, it's the responsibility of everyone on Earth and in Heaven. That's why Jesus taught us in **Mark 12:30-32: '... you must love the Lord your God with all your heart, with all your soul, with all your mind and with all your strength. The second is this: You must love your neighbor as yourself. There is no commandment greater than these.'"**

"Yes, Teacher, I obviously know that Love is what's most important. What I was referring to was Betty's unwillingness to accept it."

Yes, at first, she was unwilling. Not a lot can be accomplished with a closed heart. Many people on Earth think they practice Love or pretend to understand it, but usually, it's just on the surface. To really have a deep understanding of Love, you must open your heart completely to God and others. It must be unconditional, like a child's Love.

"So ... when Betty finally opened her heart, she was able to feel God's Love for her."

Precisely, Anabeth.

"And that allowed her to see that it was necessary to change her ways in order to truly have Love in her life."

Bingo, Anabeth. I'm very proud of how quickly you are understanding and learning.

"Thanks, Teacher! I'm really enjoying the story. Let me guess, Big John was next."

Right again, Anabeth. How did you know?

"Because he seems the most likely candidate for the next logical lesson: to Give."

Yes, Anabeth, that's correct ... but first I took a nap.

CHAPTER 12: GIVE

It was after 2 a.m. when I wrapped up with Betty and decided to get some rest.

"But you're an Angel. You don't need rest."

That's correct, Anabeth, but remember, I had taken human form, so I was experiencing everything a human does, including fatigue.

"Oh, yeah. That makes sense."

Having long, tenuous conversations was very draining to my human body, not to mention the fact that everyone else was already asleep. They were mostly propped up against the walls or their bags, trying to get as comfortable as possible, despite the surroundings. I decided to do the same. I found an open spot on the floor and sat down. I wanted to offer a short prayer prior to going to sleep.

"What did you pray for this time?"

Well, Anabeth, let's see. I thanked God for everything that had transpired so far. I thanked Him for giving me the proper words, the courage, the strength, and the faith to help everyone. I prayed that I would be able to help those who were left and for the intentions of all those who I had already spoken with. I may have prayed for more, but that's all that comes to mind right now. I do remember that it was slightly chilly in the elevator, but the praying actually warmed my heart, which helped warm the rest of my human body.

I don't know how long I slept, but I do remember waking up. Mainly because it was to the sound of very loud snoring coming from Big John. He was completely slumped back against his metal briefcase. His cowboy hat covered his face but did nothing to diffuse the sounds coming out of him, which were as loud and powerful as you might expect from a man of his size. It sounded like a steam engine locomotive traveling over rolling hills. At the apex of each hill, the loudness of each snore would increase, but the speed would slow down. As the locomotive headed back downhill, the speed would increase, but the volume would diminish. It was both loud enough to wake me but rhythmic enough to keep baby Jo asleep.

"One of the many strange sounds humans can make."

Yes, Anabeth. That wasn't the only strange sound I heard in the elevator that night ....

"Ew, gross!"

Possibly, but let's get back to my story.

As I was saying, I had awoken to Big John's rhythmic snoring to see everyone was still asleep. I pondered what my discussion with Big John would be like as I waited patiently and prayed for just a few more minutes. It wasn't long before he took an extra-long inhale, and one of his loud snores jolted him awake. His eyes snapped open, and he went from completely asleep right back to his alert cowboy self in just a matter of seconds.

"Did my snoring wake you, Ezra?" he asked with his usual southern charm.

"Oh, no. Not at all," I reassured him.

"Good, good. I have sleep apnea, and I obviously don't have my CPAP machine, so it was probably pretty bad."

"Not really. If anything, it was kind of rhythmic. I think it's helping to keep baby Jo asleep and maybe some of the others."

He laughed, deep and brisk, just like you might hear from a cowboy in an old western as he straightened out his hat and placed it on his head. "No one's ever said that before, but I reckon it could be true. I'll have to tell my girlfriend. She always complains about it. I noticed you speaking with a lot of the others. Have you gotten any sleep yourself, Ezra?" he asked with sincerity.

"Oh, yes. I was sleeping too and had already woken before you did. I just had my eyes closed to pray for a bit."

"You do that a lot, don't ya?"

"You mean pray?" I answered, wanting to be clear on where the conversation was heading.

"Yeah, pray. You forced us all to pray earlier, and here you are just a few short hours later doing it again," Big John answered, as if my behavior was abnormal.

"Yes, John, I do pray quite often. It's very comforting for me."

"I can think of many things that are a whole lot more comforting than that. Like a tall glass of whiskey, or how 'bout a nice tall blond?" He nudged me with his elbow and chuckled.

I chuckled right back, but just enough to show acceptance of his joke—not of his beliefs.

"You don't strike me as much of a drinkin' or ladies' man, Ezra."

"No, I guess not. I'm more of a spiritual person," I responded, trying to get our conversation back on track.

"Huh. You tend to hear that a lot these days. My girlfriend is always wanting me to connect with her on a spiritual level. I think it's a whole lot of mumbo jumbo, myself. I'm not really into all that spiritual crap." He flashed me an irreverent grin.

It was tempting to address his comment head-on, but I tried to gain a little more insight into his beliefs first. "What is it about your girlfriend's request that you don't like?"

"It's not that I don't like her request, I just don't see the need for it. I mean, can't we just connect in the bedroom?" He chuckled at his own joke.

"That's one way to connect, John, but I think she's looking for something different."

"Yeah, yeah, I know. We've discussed it before. She told me I don't put enough effort into our relationship. That I just get what I can out of it and don't take care of her needs. I don't know what she wants." He threw his hands up in the air before continuing. "I put her on my credit card, I pay for her apartment, her car note … I've given her all sorts of expensive gifts, but it's never enough for her. It's plum-confusing, honestly."

"What did she say she wants more of, John?"

"Oh, you know, she wants to spend more time together. She wants me to share my feelings more and to not focus on work when we're alone. All the usual female stuff."

There was a common theme in what she was looking for, but John wasn't ready to go there yet, so I sought to learn more about him. "It sounds like she really cares for you, John. How do you feel about her?"

He was quick to respond. "I care for her too. I mean, we've been together for almost five years. I'd probably marry her if it weren't for all the legal rigmarole we'd have to go through with my oil company, and all. That still comes first. Gotta protect that, even from her." His face grew serious as he mentioned his company as if he kept that in a whole separate part of his heart.

I knew I needed to learn more about the oil company if I was going to connect with him. "I can tell your company is very important to you, John."

"Ain't that the truth!"

I continued, "You mentioned earlier that you started your company about fifteen years ago. Tell me more about that."

He cleared his throat as if preparing to give a speech. "I can tell you all sorts of things about my company. She's my baby, my pride and joy. I like to call her that, seeing as I don't have any kids and never will." I looked at John with a hint of surprise at that comment, so he elaborated. "Don't get me wrong, Ezra. I love kids, and so does my girlfriend. It's just we're both too old for that now if you know what I mean." We both nodded in understanding. John continued, "You sure you want to keep hearing all of this?"

"Most definitely, John. I find it interesting. Plus, it will help me learn more about you too."

"Okay. Well, I started in the oil business right out of high school about twenty-five years ago, working for my daddy. He was a life-long rig worker, with all kinds of experience. He wasn't too much for the family stuff, but he loved work. He taught me everything he knew from day one. I was a pain-in-the-ass teenager, but I was hungry. I pretty much listened to him and learned all I could every day." He glanced down at the carpeting. "After my daddy passed on, it just wasn't the same."

"I'm sorry, John. How long ago was that?" I asked with as much empathy as his strong personality would take.

He was seemingly unaffected as he continued. "When I was almost thirty. So, I guess about fifteen years ago. Anyway, I had begun to love the oil business in my own way, so I kept on working. When the owner of our company was set to retire, I saw it as an opportunity to start my own business."

"I see. Did you buy his business to get started?"

"Heck, no! He wanted too much money. I had saved a little but not nearly enough. I lived kinda high on the hog back then, if you know what I mean. Besides, I figured with him retiring, it would be easy enough to take all his customers."

"Really? That's interesting." I replied in a completely nonjudgmental tone. Still, it was apparent John had some lingering guilt from his actions.

"Don't worry, prayer-boy. It was all perfectly legal. The old owner was the one with all the customer relationships. He kept them so close to the vest, never letting us get involved. So, when he left, the customers didn't know or care for anyone else. They were lookin' to leave. Once I came in with my shiny boots and southern charm, it was like shootin' fish in a barrel. They practically begged me to come on with my company."

"Wow. It sounds like you had a golden opportunity."

"Don't get me wrong, Ezra. I worked my tail off for many years and still do to this day. That's what you do for your baby," he said with fierce determination.

"That's a good story, John. Thank you for sharing it with me," I said with sincerity.

"I told you it was a lot." His voice nearly overflowed with pride.

"Oh, I bet a ton goes into owning a company." I nodded with appreciation for his efforts.

"Heck ya, it does! I could go on for hours more about all the employee issues, legal problems, and government regulations, but you don't want to hear any of that. Besides, that's not important. What's important is that my company is worth over $100 million." His chest swelled with pride.

"That's definitely an accomplishment, John," I said, affirming his placement of value in his wealth.

"I've had a few offers to sell, but I ain't ready for that yet. I figure I've got about ten more years to build it up. Then, I can sell it for $1 billion."

"That's quite a goal, John."

"Yeah, money is nice, but you can always have more," he said with a smirk.

"What are your plans when you reach your financial goal?" I inquired, arching my eyebrows in curiosity.

"I dunno. Maybe sit on a beach somewhere drinking a

cold one. I haven't planned it out too much yet. My girlfriend thinks I should retire now, but I just keep on working."

I gave him another inquisitive look, so he knew I wanted to know more. "Let me guess, you're one of those 'goal people,' aren't you, Ezra?"

"Goal people, John? What do you mean?"

"You know, one of those people who says you have to have goals for everything you do. That you have to write them down and then check them off as you go along to stay accountable." John put air quotes around the last word.

"Sure, goals are important," I said offhandedly. "They help define where you are going. I was more wondering what your plans for all that money are."

"Plans? I plan to spend it! I want to enjoy the fruits of my labor."

I slowly nodded in quasi-agreement. "Of course. It would be a well-deserved retirement. It's just a lot of money, and you mentioned you don't have any children, so do you plan to leave any—"

"Now don't you go using the 'C' word, Ezra!"

I blinked in surprise. "Excuse me?"

"Charity! I can't stand that word. It took me years to earn that money. I'm not just going to give it all away like that."

John was strong in his words, almost angry. I knew this was a difficult subject for him that we would have to broach before the night was over. I decided to approach things from a slightly different angle. "I've never heard of charity being called the 'C' word. That's a good one, John," I said with a slight chuckle.

"I was actually wondering more about what type of legacy you might want to leave."

John sat silently, looking as if he'd been asked a question by the teacher and didn't know the answer, so I decided to simplify things for him. "What I mean, John, is that a lot of successful people like you tend to work and create for more than the money or accomplishment. They build up something for reasons bigger than themselves. That is what becomes their legacy."

I could see John was racking his brain, trying to think of an acceptable answer. Something that would make him look good or show he had a true sense of purpose. He finally spoke, though he seemed a bit dubious. "I've never really thought about it that way. When I started my company, it was because I felt I could do things better than the old man, and I did. I grew it way larger than he ever could and made a lot more money in the process."

"Money can be a way to define success in this world for sure, John. You've already accomplished that and will no doubt have success for years to come. Let's help you define your legacy."

"Okay." He nodded with some interest.

"With regards to your legacy, what drives you to keep working today and will for the next ten years?"

"What drives me? I've always thought about it in terms of money. The more I had, the more I could grow my company and make it more successful." He smiled with satisfaction.

"So, are you driven by the growth, then?" I pressed.

"Yeah, that would be it, if you're referring to something other than money."

"Okay." I considered for a minute. "So, let's forget about the money for a second."

John's eyes swelled. "*What?*"

I raised my hands slightly. "Just hear me out, and you'll understand."

He squinted at me a little but nodded in agreement.

"Based on the current size of your company, you have enough wealth currently that you would never have to work another day in your life and would still be comfortable, correct?"

"Yeah, I guess that's true." He nodded.

"Yet you said you still want to work for another ten years to grow your company to ten times its size and value."

"Yeah, that's right."

"Then during those next ten years, if your company is growing like it should, would you work whether you were paid to or not?"

"If you put it that way, then I guess the answer is yes." He nodded firmly. "Yes, I would keep working."

"Good," I said. "You're on track for defining your legacy."

John was very engaged, as this wasn't the type of conversation he was used to having. I kept right on challenging him. "We've established that growth is important to you—or, said another way, building something so it grows is more important than the money."

John blew out a thoughtful breath. "Okay. I'll agree to that for the purpose of conversation."

"Good, then wouldn't it be beneficial to have something other than your company to help build so it can grow and flourish?"

"Something besides my company?" His eyes gleamed with excitement. "I think I'd like that!" Before I could respond he chimed back in. "It would have to be something that I really enjoy and something that I can control. You know, be the boss, like I am now."

"I completely understand, John. You've been the boss for a long time, and you're good at it."

"That's right!"

"You're also good at growing something until it's bigger and more successful."

"That's right too!"

John was very agreeable at this point due to my compliments. I kept on helping him toward his needed destination. "Then how about you start a new endeavor where you can **GIVE** to those who are less fortunate to you?"

He looked at me with one eyebrow half-slanted, as if to say he wanted to know where I was going but wasn't sold yet. "What kind of endeavor we talking about, Ezra?"

"That's entirely up to you, John. What do you enjoy doing, besides working on growing your company?"

"My company has always been my baby, but if I had to name something else, it would be my ranch. I love spending time there. Riding horses and tending to the animals … that really makes me feel alive."

I smiled. "I bet. Tell me more about it."

His face grew blissful. "Oh, it's wonderful, Ezra. It's just over one thousand acres in North Texas. It's a fully working ranch with all types of livestock, especially horses. There's over a hundred."

I looked impressed. "Wow, that's a lot of horses."

"Yeah. It's more than I wanted, but they came with the property when I bought it a few years ago. It used to be some type of equine therapy place for kids that didn't make it and ran out of money. They foreclosed, so the bank took it over, and I got a smoking deal when I bought it."

I was careful not to show my emotions at that sad news. "Sounds like you were lucky on that one. Do you know what happened to the equine therapy service?"

"Nah, not really. I got some papers about them the other day, but I don't know if they're in business anymore. My lawyer would know more about that than me. Anyway, my girlfriend and I get out to the ranch as often as we can and ride horses in the open plains. I really feel alive when I'm out there, and so does she."

"That sounds awesome, John. How often do you share the experience with others?"

He shrugged. "Not as much as I'd like, 'cause the place is huge. We usually invite other couples along when we go, and we had a big family reunion a couple years ago, but that's it."

"You ever have any children visit the ranch?" I inquired.

"Not really, although we had a whole mess of them there for the reunion. I have a lot of cousins, and they all have a bunch of kids."

"I bet the kids really enjoyed your ranch."

"Oh, yeah! They all got to milk the cows, feed the chickens, and ride horses—especially ride horses! We had big campfires at night, where they roasted marshmallows, made smores, and

I told ghost stories that made them laugh. They all had a lot of fun. I remember seeing many little smiles that week." His face lit up at those memories.

"It sounds like they weren't the only ones who had a lot of fun that week." I nudged his shoulder.

"Yeah, I guess I had fun too. I really enjoyed having all the kids around. My girlfriend keeps telling me we should do it again, but I keep putting her off 'cause of work. Maybe I'll stop delaying and get something scheduled."

"That sounds like a great idea, John." The smile grew on my face. "It also sounds like you have found your legacy."

"*Huh?*" John looked puzzled once again. He couldn't see it yet, but he would shortly. "What do you mean? What legacy?"

"Your ranch, John. Your ranch is what you can **GIVE** as your legacy."

He squinted once again." "What do you mean? **GIVE** to who?"

"I don't mean for you to **GIVE** away your ranch. I mean for you to **GIVE** the experience to others who would otherwise never have such an opportunity without your help."

He frowned and shook his head. "Who are we talking about exactly?"

"We established that you are looking for a new endeavor that you can put all of your business skills into. Something that you enjoy, that you can grow and see flourish."

"That's right."

"Your ranch provides the opportunity to do all of those things."

John was nodding in agreement—he was almost there. We just had to connect the dots a bit further. "John, you mentioned that your ranch used to be a place for equine therapy for kids. You also mentioned that you loved having all the children there for your family reunion, and lastly, you shared that you and your girlfriend were too old to have children of your own."

"Yeah, I said all that," he said slowly.

"Then why not open back up the equine therapy and bring a whole mess of children into your life! Why not **GIVE** them all the love you've been giving your company and reap rewards far more valuable than money?"

John was nodding continuously and then stopped abruptly. He looked me square in the eye and said, "You a businessman, Ezra? 'Cause that's a million-dollar idea! If I were at an auction, I'd be yelling 'sold' right now!"

"I'm glad you feel that way, John." I matched his broad grin. "So, tell me, what do you like about my idea?"

"Everything! I get to spend all my time at my ranch, I get to enjoy the children, I get to make my girlfriend happy, and I get to take over another company."

"Oh No! He didn't get it yet, did he?"

Not yet, Anabeth, but he would soon enough.

"Whew! Thank goodness!"

Thank goodness, indeed, Anabeth.

John was very close but was still thinking in terms of what he was getting and not what he was Giving. I had to get him past that for him to truly impact others. So, I used an example from Earth's history I thought would resonate with him. "John, those things are all true. Try thinking about it in terms of what you can **GIVE** to others and not what you can get."

John gave me that *But, Teacher, I don't know the answer!* look again.

"Let me use your words to explain what I mean, John. You get to **GIVE** your ranch a new purpose. You get to **GIVE** a wonderful experience to children who need it. You **GIVE** your girlfriend the gift of your time and the enjoyment of the children. Finally, you **GIVE** the equine therapy company new life."

"Boy, Ezra. Hearing you say it that way sounds loads better. My way sounds kind of greedy. I don't want to sound that way. My girlfriend always tells me she can't stand greed. She says it's the scourge of the Earth."

"Your girlfriend has a good point, John. What people often don't realize is that when you **GIVE** you get back in abundance."

"Is that so?" John commented, half-convinced.

"Absolutely, John! There are many examples of this throughout the world of business. Have you ever heard of Andrew Carnegie?"

"Yeah. I know his story. He was the richest man in the world at one point. Made his money in steel a long time ago."

"Yes, John, that's correct. He was a very successful businessman like yourself and extremely wealthy. What you may not know is that he spent the first half of his life building all his wealth and then spent the second half as a philanthropist giving it all away to those in need."

John looked thoughtful. "Wow, I didn't know that."

"There are many other stories like that, but I prefer the ones from the Bible," I said.

"I figured you would get to that, prayer-boy," he remarked with a playful wink.

"I know you're not a big Bible guy, John, yet it's easy to see the correlation to your situation when you read **Acts 20:35: 'In every way I have shown you that by hard work of that sort we must help the weak, and keep in mind the words of the Lord Jesus who himself said, 'It is more blessed to give than to receive.'"**

"You're right. That is pretty accurate," John admitted. "I've put in a lot of hard work, so you're saying I need to help the weak?" he inquired in a more serious tone than I had ever heard from him.

I responded with equal sincerity. "I'm saying that you have a wonderful opportunity to **GIVE** to those who need it. I'm saying you need to **GIVE** if you feel it's the right thing in your heart, not because you want to get something out of it. If you **GIVE** while focusing on others with a heart filled with love, then Giving will come naturally."

"Boy, Ezra, you really know how to make a man think. You're sharp. You'd do well in the oil business."

I smiled slightly. "I appreciate the compliment, John. However, I'm not looking for a job. I'm just hoping you understand the impact that you can have on a great number of lives with what you've built."

"I do, Ezra. I really do. I know I have a thick skull and can be set in my ways, but I know a good opportunity when I see it, and I don't mean a business opportunity. This time, I have the chance to help a whole lotta children, and it's about time I did something useful with my money."

"I'm very happy for you, John," I said, my warm smile growing.

"Thank you, Ezra. Thank you kindly," John said as he grabbed my hand to shake it firmly, as a southern man would to seal a deal. "I can't wait to tell my girlfriend about this whole legacy thing. She's going to love it."

John finished shaking my hand and then opened up his briefcase to take out a small notepad. He started scribbling away notes and drawing pictures at a feverish pace. Something had clearly sparked within him. He may have thought it was a million-dollar idea, but I knew it was something far, far greater than that. It was the power of God.

"God is Good!"

Yes, Anabeth. All the time.

CHAPTER 13: SERVE

Working with John had really bolstered my confidence. He was a tough nut to crack, as everything took a while to explain and hammer home. At that point, I figured that if I could get a message across to John, I could get one across to anyone.

"There's your younger, cocky self again!"

Ha-ha. Yes, Anabeth, you can call it that if you like. I like to think of it as a confident strut. You know, the way I see you walk around all the time with your peers.

"Ha-ha to you too, Teacher! Who's the funny one now? Did you use some of that humor to get your next message across?"

I tried, Anabeth, but it was not that easy. Mostly I prayed that I would continue to have similar success with those who still needed my help. Olivia was the next one up, and she proved to be tougher than Betty or John.

"Ooh, I can't wait to hear this!"

Olivia had woken up sometime toward the end of my conversation with John, which she had apparently listened in on. She was standing off to the opposite side doing some stretching/exercising in what limited space she had. She made eye contact with me and motioned for me to come over. I made my way as best as I could without stepping on the others who were still sleeping.

"Yes, Olivia?" I began.

She continued doing air squats as she spoke. "It looks like you got yourself a convert there."

I chuckled ever so slightly at what I assumed was a good-natured joke. "Nah. John and I were just talking about his plans for his next venture."

She seemed unconvinced. "Oh, is that it? It sounded like I heard a lot of praying."

"Praying?" I questioned. "You must be referring to the scripture I was sharing with him."

She smirked a little, still exercising. "Yeah, scripture. I heard you recite some different Bible verses with him and some of the others too."

"Yes, that's right. Are you familiar with the Bible and the verses I was sharing?"

"Not really. I just recognized them from when I was a little girl. My mother used to drag me to church and Sunday school every week."

"How nice," I replied, hoping it was the opening I was looking for.

"Actually, it wasn't." She rolled her eyes. "When I say drag, I literally mean drag. I didn't really care for it. I just went because she wanted me to. Church was her thing, but it was never mine."

"I see." I considered for a minute. "So, I'm guessing it's not a part of your life now."

"Nope, I don't have time for it. Too busy with work. I went for a while when I first got married 'cause my husband liked to, but now I'm divorced, so that's that. Besides, church was always filled with the same type of people I saw when I was at the DA's office. They all needed something, which is probably what I didn't care for about the whole thing."

I avoided the urge to address what she was saying head-on and sought to build more rapport. "Yes, I remember you mentioning that you started out at the district attorney's office at the beginning of your career. That sounds like it would be very interesting."

It was my mom's calling, but it wasn't for me. Like I said, too many people needing help without putting in any effort on their own." Her tone was almost scornful.

"I see. Didn't you say your mom worked as a DA for many years?"

"Yes, thirty-five long years," she sighed, as if the very thought was exhausting.

"Long? I thought you said she found the work very fulfilling."

Olivia scowled. "Oh, sure, she always said that to others, but I saw how tired she would be when she came home. I heard all the stories about the innocent being convicted and the guilty going free. Things weren't easy. That's what I mean by long."

I nodded to assure her I was listening, but I knew she wasn't telling the whole story and wanted to hear more.

"It doesn't seem like you agree, Ezra," she noted with what appeared to be discontent—though it was difficult to tell if her unhappiness with me was the reason for her unpleasant expression, as she had must have been on her fiftieth air squat by then.

"I'm sorry. It's not my place to agree or disagree. I just asked because I was making conversation."

"You sure are big on conversation and ask a lot of questions," she observed with barely concealed annoyance.

I smiled unassumingly. "I'm just very interested in people, that's all. I find them fascinating. I guess you could say I'm a student of the human race."

She cocked her head slightly—while still completing a squat. "I get that. I'm interested in people too. Not so much for pleasure but mainly because I have to for work. I mean, that's not my focus as much as it was when I was a DA. I work in corporate law now, though it still helps if you know who you're up against."

"That makes sense. Is that how you view your work? Adversarial?" I asked.

"Of course! I have to as an attorney. It's me against the other side." She straightened her shoulders with determination—at least as much as possible during a mid-squat.

"That's an interesting viewpoint. Did your mom look at things the same way in her career?" I asked, hoping that might help her open up more.

Olivia gave me that discontented look again. "You ask questions like my psychologist ... but I'll answer to indulge your curiosity." I smiled with gratitude. She continued without missing a beat. "My mom may have been my role model, but we are not the same. She didn't look at her work as adversarial at all but as a service of the community. She would say, 'Olivia, it's not you versus the other side. It's you seeking justice. If you do your job right, justice will be served.'"

"Teacher?"

Yes, Anabeth?

"Did you know she was going to say that?"

No, Anabeth, I didn't. Without realizing it, Olivia had just laid the groundwork with which I would start her lesson.

I knew that she had some obstacles to overcome before I could begin to teach her to **SERVE**, but I didn't know they went that far back. I had to continue to get her to open up if we were going to get anywhere, so I responded quickly. "It sounds like your mom was a smart woman who knew her work very well."

"Yep. She was the smartest person and attorney I knew. Always two steps ahead of everyone else." Olivia's eyes glowed with pride for her mother.

"It's no wonder she was your role model and the reason you became an attorney."

"In that sense, yes," Olivia said carefully.

"What do you mean by that?"

Olivia ignored my question and didn't respond. She stopped squatting abruptly and transitioned her body to a downward dog position. I didn't think much of it as first but then realized she had broken eye contact for a reason. Still, I wanted to stay on our current conversation track, so I mirrored her position right next to her in what little space I could.

"Is this how you do this stretch?" I asked, struggling to talk with my head down.

"That's sort of correct," Olivia responded while laughing as she glanced over at me.

I kept my focus on her, despite the fact that my human arms and legs were about to collapse.

"I don't think you heard me before," I gasped, limbs shaking from exertion. "I didn't understand what you meant when you said, 'In that sense.'"

"I heard you, Ezra," she replied curtly. "It's not something I really want to talk about."

"Oh, I'm very sorry, Olivia." Just then, my arms gave out, causing my face to crash down on Betty's purse, which nearly woke her.

Olivia once again laughed, only this time more loudly and with genuine mirth. I laughed at myself right along with her, which allowed us to bond in a way.

"You're kind of goofy, Ezra," Olivia remarked without malice while still laughing.

"Yes, I am!" I agreed with a chuckle. "That's not the first time I've been told that." Olivia found this even more amusing. She moved out of her downward dog stretch and sat cross-legged.

"Now that position looks a lot more my speed," I said confidently as I once again mirrored her. She smiled, this time meeting my eyes, the mask she had been wearing to hide her true self now absent.

"I said, 'in that sense,' because growing up, my mom wasn't just my role model, she was my superhero, my rock. She was always there for me. I looked up to everything she did with amazement and wonder like she was on top of the world … and she was, in my eyes and in the eyes of those she worked with. She was unstoppable as a district attorney, the best in the state," Oliva said with excitement and pride.

"She sounds like she was an amazing woman," I said as I reached out to touch Olivia's shoulder to offer condolences of a sort.

Olivia accepted it with a smile before responding, "Oh, she's not dead. She's just not the woman she used to be."

I nodded uncomfortably, not knowing what to say at that moment.

"She has Alzheimer's, Ezra," she explained. "That's what makes her not so super anymore."

I frowned sadly. "Oh, I see."

"It came on pretty early onset when she was around sixty, and it's gotten worse each year. Most of the time she doesn't recognize me anymore."

"I'm sorry," I consoled gently. "I bet that's very difficult."

"Yes … it is. You'd think it would get easier with time, like most things. But not this. This just gets harder and harder. Sometimes I just wish it would be over for her," she confessed with uncomfortable authenticity.

I nodded. "I understand. We never like to see our loved ones suffer."

"But that's the thing, Ezra. She's never really seemed like

she was suffering. That's how it's been the whole time. Even now, she's blissful and happy. When she was first diagnosed, she took it in stride. Never complaining about it and going on with her life and career as best as she could for a long time."

"That sounds like a great attitude to have in that situation," I said.

"*No*, it wasn't!" Olivia argued vehemently. "She continued helping others and didn't focus on herself like I thought she should. She said it was her duty. In the end, what did it get her? Nothing. She was cast aside by her job after thirty-five years of service without so much as a thank you. They even tried to cancel her pension and insurance a few years ago because the medical bills got too high. I pay for most of it now. What a slap in the face. All that service for nothing!"

Olivia had laid it all out there and was pretty fired up at this point. I struggled, not knowing whether to let her cool off or continue working on her problem. Quickly, I prayed for guidance. The first thought that came to mind was: To show her how to **SERVE,** I would need to continue to **SERVE** *her* as best as I could. I decided to take the difficult road with God's guidance.

"Olivia, you clearly love your mother very much. She has always been there for you, and you have always been, and continue to be, there for her."

"Yes," Olivia responded as if I was stating the obvious.

"And you have always wanted to support her in any way possible, correct?"

"Of course!"

"Then why did you not support her when she continued to **SERVE** others?"

Olivia straightened up and switched over to what I could only assume was her courtroom voice. "Now that's different. She didn't need to **SERVE** others anymore. She had done it long enough."

I matched her tone. "Long enough by whose definition?"

"*Mine!* I knew what was best for her at that point. She was sick and didn't know."

"You said she continued to work for a long time. How can you be sure of what you're saying, Olivia?" I said in a softer tone, trying to keep things from escalating further before continuing, "How can you be sure she wasn't doing exactly what she had done her whole career because that was what she knew best and enjoyed?"

Olivia paused for a second as if searching her mind for the right courtroom rebuttal. She remained still for a dramatic pause before responding in a way that really surprised me. "How can I be sure, you ask? Because she told me exactly what you said. She said it was her life, and nothing was going to change it. She told me multiple times to just let her be. All I wanted to do was help her win the fight, but she wouldn't let me!" Olivia was visibly holding back tears at this point.

I reached out to her and said, "Sometimes the best way to help someone is through love and support of their actions. It's not always our job to fix them or offer more than that."

Olivia was not going to give in that easy. "That might be true in a lot of situations, but it wasn't in my mom's case. She clearly wasn't thinking clearly, or she would have agreed with me."

"What makes you say that?"

"Because she always agreed with me!" she all but yelled. "She always took my advice when I offered it. We were always on the same page."

"Did you always take her advice when she offered it?" I inquired.

"When I was younger, for sure, but later in life, I started thinking for myself."

I nodded. "When did you make this change?"

"Oh, I know exactly when everything changed."

"Really, when was that?" I questioned, hoping to gain an important piece to Olivia's puzzle.

"It was when I switched to corporate law. My mom wanted me to stay in the DA's office. She said I hadn't given it enough time, that if I just worked a little longer, I would start to have the feelings toward service that she did. She said that once I started handling cases on my own, I would definitely find the joy in serving others."

"What did you think about her advice?"

"Honestly, I didn't think much about it at all. I was ready to start making money, and that wasn't going to happen in the DA's office—and I told her as much. She was very unhappy about my decision and said she couldn't support me in my choice, but it didn't matter to me. I took the corporate road and never looked back."

"So, you did what you felt was best for yourself in that situation?"

"Damn right!" she snapped, as if hammering a witness.

I was strong in my response as well. "Olivia, I can tell that you and your mother are very alike, as I'm sure you would agree?"

She nodded.

"Okay, and you are clearly both very intelligent women."

"That's right!" she affirmed, but this time with a slight grin of extra approval.

"Great. Then tell me, how is what you did any different than how your mother acted in her situation? She also did what she felt was best for herself, just as you've done," I continued before she had a chance to respond, but I kept my tone soft and calming. "You see, Olivia, you weren't upset at your mother for not taking your advice. Heck, you would have done the same thing in her shoes. What you were really upset about was that your superhero was being taken away, and it was completely out of your control. You were struggling, and not even your strength and intelligence could solve the problem." I extended my arm to take her hand as I said, "Olivia, it's okay to be vulnerable sometimes."

Olivia giggled softly and nervously while shaking her head back and forth. "Like I said, just like my therapist."

I didn't know how to take that, so I smiled back. She continued nodding and thinking for a few seconds. "You know what really gets me about the whole situation, Ezra?"

I opened my eyes wide, leaning in and waiting.

"You're right," she began. "It did bug me that I couldn't fix things, but what bothered me even more was feeling like I let my mom down."

Finally, we were getting somewhere. I needed to find out more. "In what way, Olivia?"

"I feel like I let her down by not taking her advice. By not staying a DA and serving others like she always did. If I had, maybe I would have eventually felt the kind of satisfaction she always found in her work, and we could have stayed connected till the end." She shrugged and then dropped her head as if somehow defeated.

"Olivia, your mother raised you to be the wonderful woman you are today. Nothing will ever change that. What you can change, though, is how you feel about her beliefs, even now, whether you think she realizes it or not. If you truly want to support your mother and support everything she worked her whole life for, then you can support her belief to **SERVE** others."

"I never thought of it that way. I've always thought that It was either her way or my way. We agree or disagree. I hadn't thought about supporting her beliefs."

"Olivia, you're a lawyer through and through," I said with a smile. "You're used to things being one way or another in your line of work. Things don't have to be that way in relationships. Relationships need not be adversarial. They are about **Loving, Giving,** and **Serving** one another. Remember how your mom looked at her work—not as adversarial but as a way of Serving others."

Olivia raised her head as a few tears slid down her face. "I love my mom with all my heart. I never wanted things to be adversarial with her. I want to support her and her beliefs."

"You can," I assured her. "You can support her and yourself by embodying her beliefs."

Olivia leaned forward. "What do you mean, Ezra?"

"The best way to do so is with your actions, Olivia. Look, I'm not suggesting you change careers. I'm just suggesting you view your work and life through a new lens. One that your mother would use on a daily basis."

She nodded slowly. "I think I can do that. I mean, I looked at things the way she did for a lot of my life. I just need to find that view again."

"That's great!" I cheered. "I know you will. A good place to start is in your work. In fact, it even says so in **1 Peter 10: 'As each one has received a gift, use it to serve one another as good stewards of God's varied grace.'** I'm sure you remember that from one of those times you were dragged to Sunday school, right?" I said with some quick nods and a smile.

"Okay, okay, Ezra, I understand. Let's not have too many changes all at once," Olivia said with a genuine smile.

"You're right, of course," I agreed. "I just remember that you shared that your mother was a religious woman, so that would be another way to support her and her beliefs." I winked at her.

"I know. I really do want to support her."

"I know you are being sincere, Olivia. Just make sure you take your mother's mantra to **SERVE** others as your own. Do this in all that you do, and things will go just fine!"

Olivia sighed positively and then took a couple of deep yoga breaths. "Boy, I thought only a long workout would make me feel this worn out. This was tough."

I patted her on the back. "I know. Thanks for joining in on a workout that was more my style."

She laughed. "You're welcome, Ezra. I enjoyed it, but I think I'll continue my yoga, meditate a little bit, and get some rest now."

I grinned. "You got it. Maybe we can try that downward dog again a little later," I suggested with a chuckle.

Olivia smiled warmly as she closed her eyes and continued her deep yoga breaths.

I too closed my eyes and began to pray. I thanked God for the ability to **SERVE** Olivia in the way that she needed. I prayed that she would continue to think about our conversation and possibly want to speak more at a later time. I felt we had made a lot of progress already and that she could learn to **SERVE** at levels even beyond those of her mother. Still, I knew things happen on God's time and simply thanked Him for everything that had transpired and everything yet to come in the future.

"So that's what a lawyer is like … I would always wonder when I heard an old joke and didn't fully understand."

That's funny, Anabeth. They're not all so difficult. Most humans want to do the right thing. They do try very hard and succeed a lot of the time. When they don't, they need a nudge. Luckily, I was there to do some more nudging.

CHAPTER 14: FORGIVE

By now we had been stuck together for many hours. I wasn't exactly sure what time it was but figured a cock would be crowing sometime soon, or at least building security would arrive and realize we were trapped inside and let us out. My work was still not complete, yet I did not want to rush anything.

"It couldn't be that difficult. There was only one person left."

Yes, Anabeth. Only one person remained for me to speak with, but there was a lot of work yet to be done. Time was not my main concern, knowledge and perseverance were. I felt strongly in my heart that God would give me both of those, along with the right message to finish helping those in need.

"Luckily, you had already built some rapport with Faith earlier in the elevator. She's the one you needed to help next, right?"

Yes, Anabeth, that's correct. It was Faith, and trust me, it took plenty of faith in God to help us through the conversation we were about to have.

"Nice pun, Teacher."

Ha-ha. I try.

At this point, the elevator was growing livelier. A few people had woken up and were interacting. Carly was changing

Jo's diaper, and Matt was once again helping her. Big John was asking Adam and Eva for their opinions on an idea. It looked like Betty was showing Percy and Joshua something on her phone, but she may have been asking for their help. In any case, it was nice to see everyone a bit more relaxed with one another. Faith was sitting by the door with her eyes closed and earbuds in her ears. I knew she wasn't asleep and figured she was listening to some music because she was kind of bopping her head to the beat and dancing in place. I found a spot on the floor in front of her and tapped her on the tip of her shoe.

Startled, she looked at me as if having forgotten she wasn't alone in the elevator. "Oh, hi, Ezra. Is my music too loud? I can turn it down if it's bothering you."

"Oh, no, not at all," I assured her. "I promised you I would check back in on you to see how things were going."

Her eyes opened a bit wider. "That's right, you did say that." She removed her earbuds, crumpled them up, and stuffed them in the pocket of her denim jacket.

"You sound a bit surprised," I remarked.

"Oh, I don't mean anything bad toward you! I'm just not used to people keeping their word around me."

"I'm sorry to hear that, Faith," I said gently. "That must be tough."

"Sometimes, I guess. I've gotten pretty used to it." She pursed her lips thoughtfully. "I think I just stopped expecting anything different."

"That's unfortunate. Trust is such a vital part of all relationships," I commented, hoping she would put some trust in me.

"Maybe *your* relationships, but not mine." She slumped forward a little.

"It sounds like you have some difficult ones. We can talk about that if you like," I suggested, putting as much openness into my voice and expression as I could.

"Um … okay … You were easy to talk to earlier."

I could tell she wanted to talk but wasn't quite ready to open up. "How about this?" I offered. "Let's say a prayer for you first, and then you can decide if you want to talk more about it. Fair enough?"

She smiled warmly. "Yes, Ezra. I'd like that. You said such a nice prayer earlier."

"Thank you for the compliment, Faith. That reminds me, weren't you going to practice praying on your own?"

"Oops. Yeah, I said that but I haven't had a chance to," she replied as if scolded.

"Don't worry about that, Faith. No judgment from me. I was just wondering if you wanted to give it a try first?"

"*Me?*" she responded as if just called to the front of class to solve a problem on the chalkboard. "Uh … I don't know. I mean, I don't know where to start."

Clearly, she was a little scared. I answered quickly to diffuse her fear. "I know what you mean. I used to struggle with the same thing a lot until I got more comfortable with it."

"How did you become comfortable with praying?" Faith asked with genuine interest.

"I'm not gonna lie. It didn't happen overnight. It took a long time and a lot of practice."

"That sounds pretty hard." She looked a little dejected.

"Not at all! That's the beauty of it. God is available all the time. You can practice whenever you want, and He will always be there to listen. Plus, there's never any judgment of good or bad from Him, only His welcome ear, ready to hear your prayers."

She perked up once again. "When you say it like that, it sounds really nice and comforting."

"It is! Remember I told you earlier that I keep praying in all situations because it simply makes me feel better?"

"Yes, I do remember. That's why I said I would give it a try."

"Exactly!" I nodded enthusiastically. "The very reason you are afraid and unsure about prayer is why you would benefit from more of it. Once you start praying, you will feel better. Once that happens, you will want to pray more often. And once you pray more often, you will be more comfortable with it, and it will eventually come so naturally that you'll pray all the time, every chance you get."

"Really? That will happen?" she inquired with real hope in her voice.

"Absolutely, Faith! God gives the best guarantee possible—His grace through His Son Jesus Christ, who died to save us all. Just think of your namesake if you ever forget. You can always put your *faith* in God, *Faith*."

She rolled her eyes at my corny joke as only a teenager could and then cracked a smile. "Okay, Ezra. I'll give it shot. So, *how do I start again?*"

I smiled, remembering how challenging prayer was for me

at one time. "Let me share with you what I used to do when I struggled to find the words to begin."

"Please, do!" she responded emphatically.

"I would first thank God, and then I would simply tell Him exactly what I was praying about."

Her face scrunched in confusion. "Huh?"

I shook my head at my own lack of clarity to put her at ease and then shared, "Sorry, my bad. I realize that was too vague. Let's use what you want to pray about now as an example: difficult relationships."

She nodded. "Yes, the difficult relationships I have in my life."

"Okay, so then your prayer might sound something like this: 'Heavenly Father, thank you for always being there for me. Today, I'd like to pray about the difficult relationships I have in my life ....'"

I continued, "From there, just let the words come out however they may. It doesn't matter. God will hear them all just the same."

Faith looked a bit excited. "That's it? That's all I have to do?"

"Yes, just start with that for now, and you'll do great. Don't worry if you get stuck. I'm right here to help you out."

She sat up tall as if about to give a speech. "Here goes ...." She took a breath. "God, Uh, I mean, Jesus, thank you for dying for us. I know it's been a long time since I prayed last. Sorry 'bout that. Right now, I really need to pray for the relationships in my life. They kinda suck. Oh, sorry ... Uh ... Umm ...."

I nodded, giving her a thumbs-up.

Clearly bolstered by my encouragement, she added, "I mean, they're very difficult. I hope and pray that they get better, 'cause I don't like feeling this way. Anyway, Ezra says that you can help, and I want to believe him, so … thanks."

I smiled widely and started to clap for Faith in a positive, non-mocking way. She smiled at me in return. I reached out to give her a high five, which she nearly reciprocated, then abruptly froze with her hand poised in mid-air. "Oh, shoot … I forgot 'Amen!' That's how you're supposed to finish, right?"

I laughed as I met her hand with mine, slapping our palms together. "Yes, Faith. That's the traditional way to finish a prayer. Don't worry, God will hear you just the same, whether you finish with 'Thanks,' or, 'Okay, or, 'That's it,' or whatever else. Trust me, I've used them all, although I'm a bit old-school when it comes to praying, so now I pretty much stick to 'Amen.'"

"Okay, I can do that too," she said in a simple and childlike manner.

"It really was great, Faith! I'm very proud of you. How did it feel?" I asked with sincere interest.

"A little awkward at first, but not bad at all. Not at hard as I thought."

"Good! And how do you feel about talking about your relationships now?"

She nodded, leaning toward me. "Yeah, we can definitely do that. I think it will help."

"That's great. Before we begin, would you mind if I share some scripture to start us off?"

"Sure, if you like," she answered with a little shrug, indicating she was letting me guide our time together.

I proceeded slowly, "It's a passage that will fit the conversation from **Ephesians 4:2-3: 'Be completely humble and gentle; be patient, bearing with one another in love. Make every effort to keep the unity of the Spirit through the bond of peace.'"**

Faith listened carefully. "That's pretty, but I'm not sure how it fits our conversation," she said, sounding a little unsure.

"Well, let's see. It was written by the apostle Paul when he was trying to get across some tips on how to best live as a follower of Jesus Christ. He wanted us to know that when we act in these ways, we are able to live with one another easier and have better relationships."

"Oh, I get it!" Faith chimed in before I could finish. "You chose that passage 'cause you want me to have better relationships."

"Yes, Faith, that's correct. I also chose it to give us a good frame of reference for our discussion. This way, we start out knowing that God wants us to have good and positive relationships with everyone. When we follow this scripture, we know that it is better to build someone up rather than break them down and to truly value them for who they are and not just their actions. This is how we keep the bond of peace. You see, Faith, I want all these things for your relationships, and I think you do too."

"Yes, I do want them to be positive and peaceful," Faith replied with a hint of sadness in her eyes.

"Don't worry," I assured her. "We'll figure it out, I promise. God is on your side, and so am I. Let's get started."

The Hurt and Bigger Hurt

Faith looked up, melancholy. It was difficult to tell if she was tearing up already, as she had very thick black eyeliner all around her lashes. It was clear to me that she used all that heavy makeup, along with her jewelry and clothing, to hide her true self. I figured I would fill in more of the blanks as I learned more about her. She was responding well to answering questions and seemed very comfortable with me at this point, so I continued. "Faith, I already know you have some difficult relationships, but is there one or more that you want to focus on?"

"There's a lot," she admitted with dejection. "I don't think I have one good relationship in my life right now, except for maybe my dog, Max. He always loves me, no matter what."

I smiled warmly and replied, "Dogs are great, aren't they? One of God's beautiful creations for humankind."

Faith smiled in return and was about to say something, but before she could speak, I added, "Still, I have to disagree with you about only having one good relationship. I think you actually have three." I confidently held up three fingers, which she stared at in confusion. "Max, God, and me!" I explained.

She giggled, and I affirmed my comment, "Don't ever forget that! God is and has always been there for you, and now, your new pal Ezra will be there for you too!"

Faith smiled deeply. "Okay, three it is. Now, what do we do about all the others?"

I could feel the depth of misery behind what she was saying. She truly felt all her relationships were troubled in some way.

"That's sad. I feel for her even now, as you tell the story."

I'm sure you do, Anabeth. Her emotions were very strong at the time. She was hurting. I needed to help her in every way possible. I just had to figure out how to begin. I had previously thought that relationships were the best place to start, but now I was starting to second-guess myself. I quickly ran through the options in my head. If we discussed them one by one, we might not have enough time. And, if we covered every possibility together, we might not get deep enough to really help her.

"Tough choice."

Yes, Anabeth, tough choice indeed.

"So, which way did you go?"

Well, I decided to go with a combination of both by starting with the whole, so we could later focus on the relationships that had the most impact in her life.

"Sounds like a good idea."

Thank you, Anabeth. It turned out to be.

I softened my voice and once more addressed Faith. "Tell me, Faith, would you agree that some things are missing from your relationships?"

"Absolutely. A lot of things are missing."

"Okay. I understand. If you can, think for a minute about what you feel is missing."

Faith stared off at the ceiling covered in tiny bulbs. She stayed that way for just a few seconds and then answered, "All right. I have a list in my head."

"Good. Now, tell me what's at the top of that list."

"Trust. Remember, I told you earlier that people don't keep their word with me."

I realized she was stating the obvious. "Yes, you're right. I'm sorry for not remembering that. Please forgive me."

"I forgive you, Ezra." She gave a quick shrug of her shoulders.

I gave her a fist bump to thank her for forgiving me and for shedding some needed light about her willingness to **FORGIVE**. She didn't realize it yet, but that was something that would help me help her learn to **FORGIVE** later. "You're very wise in putting trust at the top of your list, Faith."

She smiled as if I had just given her a gold star, and then waited.

"Trust is the crucial component of every relationship. It must be there if the relationship is going to flourish." She nodded in understanding as I continued. "Close your eyes and think of a relationship in which you feel trust has been broken."

"Okay." She closed her eyes, seeming to concentrate.

"Now, think back to a time where there *was* trust in that relationship."

I gave her a moment to think and then continued, "Can you feel the difference between the two?"

She nodded.

"Good. Now, visualize what each feeling looks like. If you could put a shape, color, and texture to each of the feelings, think about what that would be for each one. Make a mental picture of each ... Got it?"

She paused for a minute in deep thought. "Got it!" she finally announced. "I have a picture of each in my head. The good feeling is a bright, shiny, smooth, beautiful gold ring, and the other is a dull, rough, and ugly twisted piece of metal."

"Great. Those are very vivid descriptions, Faith. Now, think of the person attached to those feelings—the one who broke your trust. What was that person like before trust was broken, and what are they like now?"

Faith opened her eyes, which felt symbolic of her willingness to open up more. "Well, before she broke my trust, she was really loving. Always there for me. Always taking care of me."

"And how is she now?" I inquired.

"Now? Now, she's too busy with her new boyfriend. She doesn't have time for me. She feeds me and buys me clothes and stuff, but it's not the same. It's not how it used to be .... Oh, and it's my mom I'm thinking of, by the way, if you haven't figured that out, Ezra," she said as if expecting me to be disappointed.

"It's okay, Faith. I'm not here to judge you in any way. I'm only here to help you out, remember?" I smiled with gentle sincerity and extended my hand for another fist bump, which she willingly accepted. "Faith, other than some of her actions, is your mom the same person today as she was before?"

"Yes. I think so," she admitted.

"Would you say that she loves you?"

191

"Yes, definitely. She tells me so often, it's annoying." She emphasized the point with a slight eye roll.

I chuckled a bit. "Do you love her?"

The question seemed to startle her. "Of course I do. She's my mom. I'll always love her."

I responded with both a statement of opinion as well as a hint of a question. "A minute ago, when I asked you to think of how she was before and after she betrayed your trust, you described your mom's actions to define your feelings."

"Yeah, I know what you're saying," Faith said.

"You didn't describe your mom as being a different person, because she's still the same. It was only certain actions that she changed, which altered your perception of her."

Faith looked at me, obviously pondering my comments.

I paused for a while but noticed she appeared a bit stuck. "Is what I'm saying making sense?" I prompted.

"A little," she said hesitantly. "But I'm not quite sure."

"Okay. Let's go back to your mental picture of your feelings."

"Yes, my beautiful gold ring and ugly piece of twisted metal."

"Yes, that's it!" I prompted. "The pictures you have in your mind of before and after trust are two completely different objects. They are different in every way, which is why you can separate the feelings so strongly. Your mom is the same person today as she was prior to breaking trust, as you said. You are choosing to define her by her actions rather than the person that she is: your loving mother. Remember the words from our scripture: *'Be completely humble and gentle; be patient, bearing with one another in love. Make every effort to keep the unity of the Spirit through the bond of peace.'* And remember the message contained in that passage: that it is better to build someone up rather than break them down and to truly value them for who they are and not just their actions. Do you see how this relates to your situation?"

Faith's jaw dropped. "Yes, I see how it relates exactly to my situation. How did you know, Ezra? How did you pick the right message before I told you the whole story?"

I winked as I said, "Not me. God. I just shared what I thought He would want me to share. He always makes sure to get His message across. Whether we're listening or not."

Faith stared up at the ceiling again, this time as if she were looking past it to Heaven and searching for God. "Man, I really need to pray more," she realized with a slight huff—or perhaps a laugh. "That was cool how you did that."

"What's more cool is that you understand the message, Faith. So tell me, what are your thoughts about your mom's actions now?"

I expected this question to cause her to stop and think, but instead she answered immediately. "I think she just made some poor choices, which caused her to act that way. I never thought she didn't love me anymore, or anything crazy like that. I just thought she didn't care as much."

"What makes you say that?"

"Well, I think a lot of it has to do with us not spending as much time together as before. When we're together now, it always seems on edge. Meaning one of us is either rushed or not giving it what we should. This usually ends up leading to an argument of some sort."

"That sounds very challenging. I'm sure it's a struggle," I said comfortingly, hoping she would elaborate.

"It definitely is, because we don't realize it's happening until later, and by then, the damage has already been done. Our stubborn nature wins out, and we're right back at odds again. I hate it."

Faith sunk her head into her hands. I thought she might begin to cry, but instead, she quickly raised her head back up and shook it. "I don't know how to fix it. I want to change and have the relationship we used to have before … before … I mean, I just want things to get better."

I could feel the pain emanating from Faith. I knew she wasn't telling the whole story but didn't want to push too hard and risk losing the very thing I wanted to help her with: trust. I took a softer approach. "Thank you, Faith. I'm very glad you shared that."

She gave me a puzzled look. "You're welcome, I guess."

I once again laughed at myself to put her at ease. "I'm thanking you because that's exactly the attitude God would want you to have. That shows you want to choose to **LOVE** and **FORGIVE** rather than think of yourself and be stubborn. You're essentially following the advice of the scripture I read earlier. I'm very proud of you, Faith!"

She brightened a bit. "Really? I didn't even think about it. I just said what felt right."

"Beautiful! That shows that the **LOVE** in your heart is

guiding you. You're doing awesome, Faith!" I reached out, offering my half of a fist bump.

She met my knuckles with a laugh. "You really get excited about this stuff, don't you, Ezra?"

I chuckled. "Yep, this is what I enjoy the most: seeing **LOVE** in action."

"Is that what you call it? I thought we were just talking." Like your average teen, she didn't want to make a big deal out of the moment.

"Okay, okay. I know I'm a bit geeky when it comes to all this," I proclaimed as if the label were a badge of honor.

"Nah," she retorted. "I don't think you're geeky at all. I think you're just honest and truthful. You're comfortable with who you are. Most people aren't like that. I wish I were more like you."

"First off, I'll take that as a compliment. So, thank you, Faith."

She nodded and smiled.

I continued, "You're right. Many people are not like that today. Most folks feel they have to be someone else in front of others to be accepted. What is it that makes you say you wish you were more like me?"

"It's exactly what you just said, Ezra. Sometimes I feel like people won't accept me unless I act the way they do or how they want me to act."

"That's tough. How long have you felt this way?" I responded sensitively.

"Ever since ... ever since ... I mean, for a few years now.

I didn't use to be like this." She motioned to herself, hands sweeping from her hairstyle to her shoes. "I used to be more like the perfect little girl, like a little doll. People would always tell my mom how beautiful I was and that I should be in movies or modeling or something. I would never dress like I do now, with all this makeup and stuff."

"You're still a beautiful person, inside and out, Faith. No matter what type of clothing or makeup you're wearing," I replied, supporting what I hoped she knew inside. I could tell that my comment made her uncomfortable, so I quickly lightened the mood. "It's a cool look. I'm not up to date on the latest trends, but it's very goth, I think ... Right?"

She laughed at me. "Sure, Ezra, if you say so."

"What attracted you to the 'goth' style?"

She cocked her head. "Some new friends I made after I left soccer."

"Oh, yeah, I remember you said you played soccer for a long time, up until a few years ago," I recollected.

"Yeah, that's right. Soccer was my life from the time I was three. I loved it so much and still do really." She hung her head again, which I knew meant we were about to broach an uncomfortable topic.

"What caused you to stop playing?" I asked, very gently.

Faith didn't cover her face this time but hung her head even lower—perhaps shamefully. She avoided my eyes. I heard her breathing speed up.

I knew she was on the verge of letting it all out. She just needed to feel open enough to do so. I immediately prayed for God to provide some comfort for her in her time of need. Then, I extended my hand to pat her on the tip of her Converse high-top. "It's all right, Faith. You're safe. You don't have to be afraid."

Her head moved, slowly rising to reveal a face now filled with anguish. Her mascara-painted tears left black streaks down her face. "I'm scared," she said slowly. "I don't know what to do. I want to tell you what happened, but I'm ashamed."

She was trembling at this point. I tried to comfort her as best as I could. "There is nothing that can hurt you right now. It's just you and me, and God is with us. He is here to help you, and I'll do the best I can with His help." I looked deep into her eyes as I offered her my handkerchief and said, "You're safe."

Faith began to wipe her eyes. She looked around to see if anyone else was paying attention and then motioned for me to lean in closer. She brought her words up close to my ear and whispered, "I stopped playing because of some bad incidences with my soccer coach ... I mean the sexual kind of bad. He touched me inappropriately, and I didn't like it, so I quit the team." She leaned back as if one of the many weights she was carrying had been lifted. "That's all. That's my big secret. I'm not proud of, it but it's the truth."

I looked deeply into her eyes. "Faith, I'm very sorry that happened to you. That was completely wrong and unfair for him to do that to you. You are a very strong young woman, and you should be proud of yourself for the strength you had to speak up both then and today."

She smiled softly. "Thank you for saying that. I didn't get as much support from the other people I told back then."

It was a very upsetting statement, but I held back my emotions and asked, "What do you mean?"

"My parents didn't believe me at first. They thought I was just exaggerating because I didn't want to play anymore. He had been my coach for many years, and they were friends with him and his wife. They eventually realized I was telling the truth when another girl on the team shared a similar story, but that was, like, a year later." She stared at me, waiting to hear what I said next.

"I'm so sorry you had to suffer all that time, Faith."

She nodded. "Yeah, it was miserable and pretty lonely." A shadow fell over her face; it was as if she were feeling those emotions all over again.

"I'm sure it was very miserable at the time and may still be now, in some ways. But it may help if you remember one thing."

"What's that?" Her eyes were wide, hopeful, longing for something to grasp onto to ease the painful memories.

"Just know, you were never alone. I know it's difficult to imagine, but God was always there with you, even in the worst of times, just as He is today."

She glanced away. "That's what the nuns at the school said too when I was about to transfer from St. Joseph's. It's hard to believe stuff like that when it's happening, though. You're only thinking about all the awfulness that's going on."

I sighed. "Yes, people can be incredibly awful and hurtful—even those whom you trust—which I know makes it feel worse."

"You're right. It does make it worse."

"Does it still feel the same today, or has it gotten better over the past few years?"

"It's gotten a little bit better each year. I don't think about it all the time anymore like I used to. Now, I can actually be around people without feeling like all eyes are on me, judging like they know everything. Sometimes, when it gets bad, I feel very scared and ashamed, but it comes and goes."

I looked at her with deep sympathy. "I'm sure it's been difficult to carry that burden around. Have you spoken to anyone about it? Someone you trust, like a counselor?"

Faith squinted at me, looking dubious. "Right afterward, I spoke to the counselor at the school. It helped a little, but then I transferred out. After that, I just wanted to forget things, and I didn't want to tell anyone else. My mom would bring it up from time to time when she thought I was having a bad day, but that's when we started having problems, so I just brushed her off." Faith wiped her face once more and offered me back my handkerchief.

I gently pushed it back toward her. "You keep it, just in case." She did the slight eye roll again but gladly took it back with a smile.

"I know you've had a very difficult few years, Faith, and still sound like you are healing. I'm sure you would like that process to be over too."

"For sure! I don't like thinking about it, and it is definitely a burden, like you said."

"Well, I'm glad we are talking about it now. I know you

haven't had great experiences discussing it previously, but that is one of the ways to help heal."

She gave the classic teenager "I know" look, so I immediately gave her a preferable option. "There is something else you can do to help you heal. Something that is almost magical in its ability to make you feel better."

"What, *pray*? We already talked about that, Ezra. I know it will help, and I'm going to start praying more often," she retorted.

"Yes, praying will help. It can be magical in its ability to make things better. In this case, though, I'm talking about something different."

"Enough already. What is it?" she snapped impatiently.

I straightened up. "**FORGIVE**," I answered simply.

"Forgive? *FORGIVE*? Who, exactly, do I need to forgive?" Faith responded in a loud, annoyed voice.

I softened my tone to calm her. "Faith, I know that it's very difficult to hear. To **FORGIVE** those who have hurt us is one of the most challenging things we face in life. It is also one of the most liberating, rewarding, and beneficial things you can do for yourself. To answer your question of whom, the true answer is: everyone. Anyone who has hurt you needs to be forgiven in your heart for you to truly heal."

Faith looked up at the ceiling again and then back down, then started vehemently shaking her head. "I can't do it. There's no way. I don't think I'm ready for that yet."

"You may not be, Faith. Forgiveness can only happen when it is from your heart and genuine. If not, then the wounds will still be there, and they will continue to hurt. Once you can commit to fully **FORGIVE,** then you will see the magic in action. You will see that the burdens you are carrying are suddenly gone, as are the feelings of fear and shame, and you will once again feel normal."

Faith looked at me with a glimmer of hope. "That all sounds wonderful, and I do want all those things. I just know that I'm not ready to **FORGIVE** my coach."

"I understand, Faith. You will know in your heart when you're ready."

"That's it?" Anabeth asked in disbelief. *"That's all you got?"*

Not so fast, Anabeth. Wasn't patience one of the first lessons in your training?

"Sorry, Teacher. Yes, it was. I'm just very anxious to hear how things turned out."

I know, Anabeth. I was getting anxious in my discussion with Faith at that moment as well.

The Magic

While it was difficult to hear that Faith was not ready, I didn't want to force anything—especially something that would end up making her feel worse. Still, I needed to help her learn how to **FORGIVE.** Luckily, there were other examples I could use. "What about the others you need to **FORGIVE**?" I asked.

That look of surprise returned to her face. "Others? I heard you say everyone, Ezra, but I thought that was metaphorically speaking. What—I mean, who—do you mean?"

"I can easily answer your question. However, I think you would be better off searching your heart for the answer."

Faith looked at me with bewilderment. She had already been through a lot, so I gave her a little nudge with one of my favorite passages. "Faith, Let me share some scripture that I think will help. Matthew 18: 21-22: 'Then Peter went up to him and said, 'Lord, how often must I forgive my brother if he wrongs me? As often as seven times?' Jesus answered, 'Not seven, I tell you, but seventy-seven times.' What does this say to you, Faith?"

"It tells me I should forgive my brother over and over again. I don't have a brother, but I guess it means those close to me? Wait ... my mom! I need to **FORGIVE** my mom."

"Yes, Faith, that's correct! Now, tell me, what do you feel in your heart that you need to **FORGIVE** her for?"

Faith didn't look up this time, but rather closed her eyes and folded her hands in prayer. She took only a few seconds and then was ready to respond. "My heart tells me that I've been holding some things against her. Things that I blame her for. I really need to **FORGIVE** her for not believing me when I was abused, for not being there when I needed her, and for breaking trust with me. I've been blaming her for everything when none of it was her fault."

"That's some excellent insight, Faith. You are clearly wise beyond your years." I gave her another wink.

"Thank you, Ezra. That wasn't so difficult to think of, actually. It was in my heart like you said. I just didn't know it was there. The hard part will be telling her that face-to-face."

"That's true. It will be harder, but it will be real and genuine, which I know she will appreciate. You can always practice with God ahead of time. Just pray to Him and tell Him that you **FORGIVE** your mom. He will gladly accept your prayer and will help you when you are with her in person."

"Okay." She nodded. "I like that idea. I'm going to do that right now." Faith closed her eyes and clasped her hands as she held them up to her heart like a child immersed in bedtime prayers. She didn't speak out loud, just in her heart to God. I prayed along with her and for all of her intentions and for God to help her. When she was finished she opened her eyes with a big smile.

"I'm very proud of you, Faith." I smiled and nodded. "How did that feel?"

Her smile grew even bigger. "Great. It was liberating like you said. I do feel like some of the burden is gone."

I beamed; she was making great strides. "That's wonderful. Just wait till you share forgiveness with your mom. Then, you'll really feel the magic happen as the burden disappears."

Her eyes sparkled. "Oh! I wish she were here. I would do it right now."

"I appreciate your excitement, Faith. Don't worry. That time will come soon enough. There is one other person besides your mother and coach that you can **FORGIVE** to help ease the burden immediately."

Faith squinted as she thought briefly and then blurted out, "You mean, Betty—the old lady who was rude to me earlier."

I laughed quietly. "That would be nice, but she wasn't who I was referring to. The other person you need to **FORGIVE** is yourself."

Faith pointed at herself incredulously. "*Me?*"

"Yes, Faith. You have been punishing yourself for what happened to you. You thought it was your fault and felt ashamed. When you **FORGIVE** yourself, you allow yourself to be free of all of these negative feelings. You can ask God to **FORGIVE** you for putting yourself through all the pain you have endured over the past few years."

Her mouth opened slightly in surprise. "I hadn't thought of that before. I didn't know it was important to **FORGIVE** myself."

"Yes, Faith. Everything begins and ends with you. You must **LOVE** yourself always, and you must **FORGIVE** yourself when necessary. God loves you as one of his children, and He always wants the best for you. This includes to **LOVE** and **FORGIVE**, always."

"Wow! That's powerful stuff," she exclaimed. "You make God sound way more awesome than the nuns did in school."

I chuckled. "You're funny, Faith. I'm sure the nuns did a great job too, but seriously, how do you feel about forgiving yourself?"

"I'm not sure. I've never done that before. If you think it's necessary, then I guess I can do it," she replied with a shrug.

"Faith, please remember, I'm only here to help you in any way I can, to be a sounding board as you think about what has been troubling you. I'm not here to make decisions for you.

You have to do what you feel in your heart. What is your heart telling you?"

She didn't waiver this time. "My heart says that it is ready to be free of the burdens of my past. It says it wants me to be happy."

"That's great. Then ask God to **FORGIVE** you, and He will."

She paused. "Do I pray the same way I did when I prayed about my mom?"

I smiled. "Sure. Whatever comes out will be fine. Just speak to God like we're speaking now. Remember, He's a great listener."

"Okay, here goes!" Faith returned to her childlike bed-time-prayer position. She had an intense look of emotion on her face, despite her closed eyes and the stillness of her mouth. She took much longer than she had when forgiving her mom and then opened her eyes with a look of accomplishment. "I'm done. I feel really, really good about doing that!"

"That's super!" I said, filled with excitement. "I'm very happy for you, Faith." Then I noticed that she looked as if she had another question on her mind. "Is there something else you want to add, Faith?"

"Yes. When I was praying it really felt like God was here listening. I think I actually felt His presence with me. It was strange at first, but comforting, for sure. It almost felt the way it does when you haven't seen a friend in a long time, and you give them a hug. You know, you can feel how much you missed them. Yeah, that's how it felt."

"How completely beautiful, Faith! What a wonderful feeling."

"Yes, it was so wonderful that for a split-second the thought crossed my mind while I was praying to **FORGIVE** my coach," she admitted.

"I see," I replied, leaning forward and hoping things may have changed.

"I decided not to, though," she continued. "My heart isn't ready for that."

"That's okay, Faith. God will be ready when you are." I extended my hand for a final high five as if to say great job, but Faith waved it off. Before I could respond she leaned over and wrapped her arms around me in a big hug. As she did, she whispered in my ear, "Thanks for being so cool and understanding, Ezra. I think God wanted us to meet in this elevator." She pulled back, and without saying another word, took her earbuds out of her jacket pocket and placed them back in her ears to indicate she was finished with the conversation. My work with her had finished for now. I gave her a warm smile with a double thumbs-up and then closed my eyes to thank God for what had just happened.

*"All right, I'll admit it, Teacher. Being patient to hear the rest of the story was worth it. I'm glad she learned how to **FORGIVE**."*

Yes, Anabeth, so was I. Faith was able to both **LOVE** and **FORGIVE** in our short time together. It was a special time for her and me, to be sure.

*"What about her coach? Weren't you sad that she wasn't able to **FORGIVE** him?"*

Honestly, Anabeth, only for a brief instant. Yes, I did gain hope when she mentioned thinking about it, but I knew she wasn't ready. You may not have learned this yet, but when a human **FORGIVES**, it has the greatest impact when it is in alignment with God's plan. This is why I told Faith to do what she felt in her heart. If her heart was fully open to receiving God, it would be fully open to Forgiveness. She was getting there but hadn't quite gone all the way. Don't worry, Anabeth. Remember, I did say my work with her had finished, but only for now ....

CHAPTER 15:
EXPAND THE RELATIONSHIP WITH GOD

A t this point in the story, you may be thinking, *Everyone has been helped. The end is near.* That was true to a certain extent. I had helped each one of them with their immediate challenges on an individual basis. I had taught Carly to **SHOW GRATITUDE**, Matt to **BE PRESENT**, Percy to **GROW**, Eva and Adam to **HAVE FAITH**, Joshua to **PRACTICE STILLNESS**, Betty to **LOVE**, John to **GIVE**, Olivia to **SERVE**, and Faith to **FORGIVE**. One would naturally think I was nearing the completion of my elevator task, as I did. Yet, something inside told me my work was not yet complete. That something was just sitting out there, elusive in a sense. It wasn't something I felt when I was praying per se; it was like knowing I had one piece still left to place in the puzzle—a piece that wouldn't be too hard to contend with, yet I couldn't see the shape of it and didn't know where to find it. I decided to pray about my time with everyone as a whole. There were commonalities, such as all of us being stuck together and each of my fellow riders having a problem requiring my help, but there was definitely more than that. As I reviewed my time with each passenger in my mind, I kept hearing the same thing over and over again: *Follow your prayer, Follow your prayer.* It was difficult for me to discern what that meant, initially.

"I know what it means! I get why you were being told that."

Oh, really, Anabeth?

"Yes, really! God was telling you to follow the initial prayer you shared with everyone in the elevator when you first got stuck."

Yes, Anabeth, you're correct. That's what I was being told by the words: *Follow your prayer.* I just didn't realize it right away. I thought I was being taught a lesson in prayer and figured it meant I needed to keep praying for the answer. Seems silly, I know, and we can laugh about it now, but I blame it on the fatigue of being in human form.

"I guess! If that's how you want to explain it, Teacher!"

Either way, Anabeth, my eyes and heart were not fully open. It eventually clicked a short time later when I saw Faith folding her hands to pray.

It was then that I thought back to what I had said in my prayer at the beginning of this task.

As I reflected on my prayer, two parts stood out to me. First, *We make ourselves 100 percent available to the gift of your grace as we know that it was given to us through the sacrifice of your Son, our Lord and Savior Jesus Christ.* And second, *We pray that our eyes will be wide open to all your amazing possibilities.*

Both of these had been extremely important components of my time with everyone. I quickly realized that I had not helped everyone to be 100 percent open to God's grace—and everyone's eyes were not yet open to all of God's amazing possibilities.

"That's what I was thinking too, by the way."

Good, Anabeth. You've been listening very well this whole time. Keep it up!

Now that I had a clearly defined goal, I needed to come up with a specific plan to get there in a short period of time. I figured the best path was going to be to engage the group as a whole to get them sharing with one another. Then, I could show them how essential it was to have God in each of their lives. I could illustrate the incredible impact of opening one's eyes to all of God's amazing possibilities. It wasn't going to be easy, but I was ready for the task, and I had God on my side.

Even though I couldn't see the sky, I knew morning was on the horizon. Everyone was now awake, alert, and anxious to get out of the elevator, as it was just about 6 a.m., when the building was scheduled to open up. All the previous conversations had been replaced with the uncomfortable silence of anticipation of the doors suddenly bursting open.

After a few minutes of nothing happening, Big John finally broke the silence by saying, "I guess I should let you all know, in case you've never been in first thing on a Saturday morning like I frequently am, this building doesn't open till 7 a.m., seeing as today is Saturday and all."

Everyone erupted in moans and groans. Big John did his best to provide some comfort. "Well, sometimes, Franklin gets here around 6:45 a.m., 'cause he knows I'll be waiting. Maybe today is one of those times."

"Great!" an agitated Matt blurted out. "That's real comforting. A whole fifteen minutes earlier!"

Clearly irritated by Matt's comment, Big John yelled, "Now just a Goddamn minute! I'm only trying to help! We've been here this long. What's a few minutes more?"

Matt stood up and was about to get in John's face. I knew I had to interject and change the dynamic or risk losing everything I had accomplished with everyone. I stood and slid in between them with my back against the wall, where I could face everyone as I raised my hands and started to speak. "I'm sorry. I'm sorry! John, Matt, everyone, this is my fault! I know we are all tired, hungry, irritable, and ready to get out of this elevator, but it's my fault that we are stuck here for a little while longer."

Everyone looked at me with disbelief—exactly like you're looking at me right now, Anabeth. Don't worry, I didn't tell them what you think. I continued to keep my identity secret.

"That's a relief!"

Yes, Anabeth. I had a different plan, which I was ready to share with them.

First, I waited a moment to let my comment settle in and was about to explain further when Percy shouted out, "Wait! Did you break one of the buttons?"

"No, Percy, I haven't touched the buttons, or touched anything else on the elevator, for that matter. What has been touched is my heart by the warmth and kindness you have all shown me and each other during our time together. It might not have been completely obvious, but when we first got stuck I wasn't doing too well. I was frightened, lonely, and uncomfortable. You helped to take all that away and replace it with feelings of courage, acceptance, and love. I had the pleasure of speaking with each of you individually, and it was beautiful and rewarding."

Before I could finish, Eva interrupted with, "You're very kind, Ezra! We should be thanking you."

Carly jumped in. "Yeah, thank you for your help, Ezra!"

Others were about to do the same when I stopped them all. "Thank you both, and thank you all for being open to having conversations with me. Now, please, please, let me finish. It's very important." I had everyone's full attention now, which was perfect for what I was about to say. "I feel like we are still stuck here because our time together is not complete. While you all were gracious enough to pray with me earlier, I made a promise to God within my prayer. I promised him that our time together would be worthy of His presence and that it would be filled with His love and grace. I also promised Him that our eyes would be wide open to all His amazing possibilities." I paused to let them ponder those words, then, before anyone could speak, I clarified my thoughts further. "Look, I know that I wasn't just praying for myself, and I made some assumptions as to everyone wanting to be filled with God's grace. I just know the benefits of having God in your heart and being open to His possibilities, and I felt that I owed it to all of you to share that gift—a parting gift, if you will. That's what our remaining time needs to be devoted to, so each of you can understand how to **EXPAND THE RELATIONSHIP WITH GOD**."

As I finished my explanation I was met with looks ranging from confusion to apathy to hope. It was a mixed bag, to be sure. I looked around for support. Luckily, a few people had my back.

Betty kicked it off. "Ezra's right. There's no sense bickering. I've been on this Earth a long time and haven't met too many folks like him who know as much as he does about **LOVE**. I say we give him a chance."

I nodded toward Betty in thanks as Matt surprisingly spoke up next. "I agree with Betty. Pretty soon we can all go back to our lives. For now, let's all **BE PRESENT** in the elevator with one another."

I shook Matt's hand in thanks as I noticed affirming nods from Faith and Joshua from across the elevator.

Carly took the opportunity to speak next. "I would really like to say that I'm very grateful for things going smoothly last night for Jo. I think we can all **SHOW GRATITUDE** for Ezra and each other."

I kissed my finger and extended my hand to place the kiss on Jo's head, which I patted softly. Carly placed her hand on top of mine and smiled in acceptance. Support was flowing in from all over, which provided me with a welcome flood of emotion. I wanted to begin our conversation, but the emotions were somewhat overwhelming and kept me from speaking right away.

Adam was kind enough to provide a perfect segue. "Being stuck in this elevator has not been easy for any of us. It's been crammed, hot, stinky, and uncomfortable, to name a few issues. For some of us, it was a challenge emotionally as well. Eva and I were not having a very good day at all prior to getting in the elevator. It wasn't until we spoke with Ezra that we felt better and saw that we have a future. We all owe it to him to **HAVE FAITH** in what he is saying and **HAVE FAITH** that it will have a positive impact on our lives."

Eva hugged Adam with one arm and me with the other as we exchanged thanks. The stage had been set. Everyone was now more open than they had been just a few minutes prior when I proposed my idea. It was now time for them to **EXPAND THE RELATIONSHIP WITH GOD**.

Giant Baby Steps

Everyone in the elevator had some limited experience with God and prayer at some point in their life. There was a lot of variation between one another, and little in common. What everyone did have in common was a desire to have a better life in some way due to the fact that they were all lacking something. My goal was to take what I knew about each of their lives and show the value of having God a part of it. I needed to show them that in addition to the lesson I had taught each of them, that God was what was lacking. By adding God into their lives they would fill the void that they were experiencing. I knew I had to start slow, with baby steps, so I figured, why not use baby Jo to illustrate my point?

"Thank you for the kind words of support and encouragement, everyone," I began graciously. "Let me start out by saying that I'm not here to try to change anyone's beliefs. I'm only here to help you see the importance of having God in your life. To shed some light on God the way I see Him, as our loving Father who watches over us every day. A Father who sent His Son Jesus Christ to die on the cross so that we would have eternal life."

I could see that my words were a bit much for some, so I made it more relatable to our situation. "When we first got stuck, I prayed that our time would be a blessing and special. I feel that it has been for me, and I hope it has for you as well. I believe that a big part of it was God's presence here with us. I know He helped all of us make it through the night, whether we realized it or not. You see, God is working all the time, even when we don't know or think He is there. He is watching over us like a good parent and tending to us when we need it the most."

"Just look at little baby Jo. As an infant, she is innocent and fragile. Without Carly to take care of her, she would not survive. She does not fret or worry that her mother will abandon her. She knows that her loving mother provides for her in every way. She is there whenever she needs anything and will always be there no matter what."

"You got that right!" Carly chimed in right on cue.

Betty joined in to support her. "She was so good all night. We didn't even hear a peep. You're a wonderful mother!"

"Thank you, Betty! I feel very grateful to be Jo's mom," Carly answered.

I smiled at their exchange and then finished my point. "God is the same way with us as Carly is with Jo. He knows what we need better than we do. He supports us and provides **LOVE** and comfort if we allow Him to, especially in times of need. Look, all of us in here have problems we are dealing with today and every day. Oftentimes the worry consumes us and becomes more challenging than the problem itself. This will bring us way, way down if we let it. A better option is to seek God's help. This is illustrated perfectly in scripture, such as **Matthew 6:8: 'Your Father knows what you need before you ask him,'** or **Proverbs 3:5-6: 'Trust in the Lord with all your heart, and do not lean on your own understanding. In all your ways acknowledge him, and he will make straight your paths.'"**

Both passages seemed to resonate with Percy, who immediately made his presence known. "I've been relying on myself for most of my life, and it hasn't gotten me anywhere. It wasn't until now that I realized I need to start relying on God so I can begin to **GROW** in ways I never imagined."

I nodded. "That's great, Percy. I'm proud of you for speaking up. Thank you."

"No, thank you, Ezra," Percy replied in a loud, clear voice.

His newfound confidence was a surprise to everyone in the elevator, but none more than Olivia, who had dismissed him earlier. Now, it was her turn to surprise us all. "Hey Percy, any second thoughts on checking out mergers and acquisitions with my company? I bet you can **GROW** there."

Percy beamed with newfound confidence. "I'd love to check it out. Thank you for giving me the chance."

Olivia responded with a thumbs-up and sincere smile. "You're welcome. Anything I can do to **SERVE** one of my new elevator friends."

I was about to take back the reigns, but the positive inter-action just kept on rolling as Big John spoke up next. "Since you put it that way, Ms. Olivia, how about you **SERVE** some of that lawyering in my direction? I'm about to **GIVE** all that I can in a new non-profit company. I could really use some of your legal expertise."

Olivia seemed a little surprised by John's request but clearly welcomed the idea. "Of course! I did some pro-bono non-profit work when I was in the DA's office. I'd love to help. I'll even help you **GIVE** back by doing the work pro-bono."

Her words were music to Big John's ears, who outstretched his large hand to shake on the deal. Olivia gladly accepted as she looked over in my direction with a wink.

Their momentum was awesome to watch. Everyone was riding the high of being open to one another and God. They were truly being genuine in their words and actions. The timing was perfect to share some scripture to enforce the point. I was about to speak when Betty raised her arms to quiet everyone down. "Everyone, everyone, can I have your attention, please? I've been sitting here watching everything transpire, and it's been really beautiful. Isn't this a lot better than bickering with one another? And so much easier?" We all laughed. She continued, "I'm very happy Ezra got us started on the right path. I'd say our interaction with one another is a definite example of **LOVE**, wouldn't you, Ezra?"

"Most definitely, Betty!" I exclaimed. "You are all following the word of God, just like it says in **John 13:34: 'I give you a new commandment: Love one another. As I have loved you,**

so you also should love one another.' I'm very proud of all of you."

Betty was right. It had snowballed into a full-on avalanche of **LOVE**. I was thrilled that everyone was exemplifying their individual lessons and sharing with the group. The thought crossed my mind at that point that only two remained to share what they had learned.

Just as I was about to pray to prevent doubt from creeping in, Joshua spoke up. "I don't know about you guys, but I for one need to take a moment to **PRACTICE STILLNESS** and pray about everything that has just happened."

What? I thought. Had I heard him correctly? Joshua wanted to pray?

I didn't have time to doubt before Joshua added, "Come on, everyone. Let's close our eyes and take a moment to reflect on what just happened. You'll like it, I promise. As we all close our eyes, let's also pray that we can open them to all of God's amazing possibilities, just like Ezra said at the beginning." It was amazing. Joshua had come around on God's time when I least expected it. It was a small miracle—the work of God.

I watched as everyone sat still in deep thought and prayer. I too joined in and prayed that they would finally feel God in their hearts, minds, and souls. I prayed for all of them equally and then said an extra special prayer for one of them. I wasn't quite finished praying when I felt a tap on my arm. I opened my eyes to see the object of my extra special prayer, Faith, in front of me.

She pulled my shoulder to bring my ear closer to her and whispered, "I'm ready to **FORGIVE** my coach, and I want to do it now. Is that okay?"

As I pulled back, I looked deep into her eyes and saw a certainty and confidence that was undeniable. "Yes, of course, Faith. You can share whatever you are ready to."

She wrapped her arm around my neck for a quick hug and then turned to face everyone who had finished praying. "Everyone, I didn't think this would happen here, but the time is right. I've been so moved and touched by all the **LOVE** that has been shared in the elevator that I feel I need to share too. There's something I need to tell you all, something that has been weighing on me for a long time. It wasn't until right now that I realized I'm ready to let it out by sharing it with you."

A wave of encouragement flowed out from the group in various forms, which clearly had a positive impact on Faith. She thanked everyone for the support and then continued, "I am finally ready to **FORGIVE** someone who hurt me very badly. My coach took advantage of our close relationship and abused me in many ways." She paused as she started to tear up. Both Betty and Carly put their arms around Faith to support her physically and emotionally, which she welcomed gladly as she continued letting the demons out. "The pain of what happened has prevented me from being open to myself, others, and especially to God. I want to move past all that. I know now that the only way to do so is to **FORGIVE**. I know the person who harmed me is not here, and I may never have the opportunity to tell him face-to-face, but I'll share it here and now." She paused once again to take a deep breath before finally claiming her freedom. "Coach, I **FORGIVE** you. I release myself from the trauma, pain, and suffering of what happened. Coach, I **LOVE** you as a child of God and thank you for helping to make me into the person I am today."

I was speechless, having never before experienced such an extremely special act of forgiveness. I could only stand there, tears of joy and pride silently sliding down my cheeks. I wasn't the only one—there was not a dry eye in the elevator. Everyone took turns congratulating Faith and sharing more **LOVE** as we continued to bask in the gifts of one another.

My Lesson

We were in such a good place that we could have stayed in that elevator for three or four more hours and no one would have noticed. I, however, was keeping a close eye on the time as I wanted to make sure we kept the momentum up until we parted ways. I settled everyone down and got their attention. "Thank you, thank you, thank you all from the bottom of my heart! When I told you we all need to **EXPAND THE RELATIONSHIP WITH GOD,** I figured I was going to lead the discussion. Boy, was I wrong! You all clearly have God in your hearts and are filled with His divine grace. Your actions clearly show it, whether you perceive it now or are still learning. It does not matter what your individual beliefs are, you can still be open to His gifts. Not only that, I would go so far as to guarantee that He was—correction, is—in the elevator with us and has been for the past twelve hours. There is no denying this with all the magical interactions that have taken place."

I spoke to them from a place deep within my heart, where I could feel God's presence. It was resounding and strong like I had never felt before. I thought back to when I first appeared in the elevator when all the fear and doubt attacked me, and I struggled. I thought I was alone, but God was there, always by my side. It was then that I realized I needed to be taught a lesson just as much as everyone else. I believed I was teaching them to **EXPAND THE RELATIONSHIP WITH GOD** when I was actually teaching myself. You see, no matter who you are, be it human or Angel, there is always the opportunity to **EXPAND THE RELATIONSHIP WITH GOD.**

"Wow, Teacher! I didn't see that coming."

Me neither, Anabeth. While it may have been a bit surprising, it was far, far more comforting. I learned, in that instant, to never doubt the power of God. I gained true respect for His wonderful ability to know all of His children better than we know ourselves. This was part of the final piece of **EXPAND THE RELATIONSHIP WITH GOD** that I needed to share with everyone, and I knew exactly how I was going to do it.

The Golden Rule

When I confirmed God's presence to the group, they all took it with warmth and **LOVE**. We even celebrated in a sense by giving hugs and exchanging high fives, fist bumps, and pats on the back for our group accomplishment. When we had settled down, everyone looked my way, expecting me to tie a bow on our experience. I stood tall in the corner of the elevator and asked everyone to sit down for one final message. I looked from side to side, making eye contact with each one of them in turn as I said their names. "Thank you, Carly, for showing gratitude, Matt for being present, Percy for growing, Eva and Adam for having faith, Joshua for practicing stillness, Betty for loving, John for giving, Olivia for serving, and Faith for forgiving. You have all not only changed yourselves for the better but have also changed me in more ways than you will ever know. I also want to express my deepest appreciation for helping me keep my promise to God. Our time has been worthy of His presence and filled with His love and grace.

"There's just one final thing I'd like to share before we part ways that will help us have a greater impact on our families, friends, communities, and everyone else we come in contact with. If we do this one little thing, our actions will have a ripple effect that will literally **CHANGE THE WORLD**."

Their eyes lit up in magical wonder and anticipation of what I was going to say next. I motioned for all of them to move in a bit closer as I leaned in, softening my voice as if about to reveal a valuable secret, and said, **"Do unto others as you would like them to do unto you."**

At first, they all inhaled my words with awe as if never having heard them before by nodding to each other and motioning in agreement. Once it had soaked in for everyone, though, they were suddenly not so amazed.

Big John blurted out, "I've heard that one before. My mama used to tell me and my brother that when we would fight as kids."

"Yeah, that's basic Christianity 101. I think I learned that at St. Joseph's in kindergarten," proclaimed Betty.

Even Olivia commented, "My mom said she lived by that rule in her legal work."

I could see they needed a little more explanation. "You are all correct. This is not something new I am telling you. It has been around for a long time. I personally know it best from Jesus's teachings in **Matthew 7:12: 'So always treat others as you would like them to treat you; that is the Law and the Prophets.'**

But this 'Rule of Reciprocity,' or, 'Golden Rule,' as it's called, is not unique to Christianity. In fact, it can be found in all major religions and in society as well. Some of you may know it by other names, like 'Give back,' 'Pay it forward,' 'Pass it on,' or 'Love your neighbor.' No matter what you call it, the foundational message remains the same: Treat others the way you want to be treated. That's it, plain and simple."

"That does sound very simple," agreed Joshua.

"You're right, Joshua," I nodded. "But what's simple to do is also unfortunately simple not to do."

"So why don't people practice it?" asked Faith.

I shook my head a few times with uncertainty, showing how much I wished I could provide some logic before responding as best as I could, "That's a good question, Faith. I wish I knew the answer. My best guess is that most people are more focused on themselves. They are thinking, *What's in it for me?* rather than, *How can I help someone else?* A lot of people live their entire lives that way. It's unfortunate."

"Ezra's right about that! I know from experience that a life lived like that is selfish and unfulfilling. I'm glad I know better now!" pledged Big John.

"Yes, me too, John!" I smiled. "I'm glad everyone here knows better, which is why I felt compelled to share it now. All of you to this point have lived your lives in a certain way. I'm not saying it has been good or bad. I'm saying that we can all be better. We *need* to be better if we want to make the world a better place. If we practice the Golden Rule the way God wants us to, then we will **CHANGE THE WORLD**."

My message was received well by everyone and was gaining momentum—or so I thought.

"Ezra," Matt began, "I have a question."

"Yes, Matt?"

"I've been up against some pretty tough odds in my life, so I have to ask: How is my paying for a stranger's coffee in the drive-thru going to **CHANGE THE WORLD?**"

"That's a great question, Matt. I appreciate you bringing it up because I bet others are thinking the same thing." A few mutters of agreement carried across the elevator. "Here's how it works. When you do unto others by paying for their coffee, for example, it has an impact on them that you typically can never measure, but that doesn't matter. The impact is measured by the world and by God. Each time you love your neighbor by actions such as the one you mentioned, it releases the **LOVE** of God in our lives. It helps to spread the **LOVE** of God around the world one bit at a time, and it enables you and your one small action to make a difference in the world. This is what I meant when I said **EXPAND THE RELATIONSHIP WITH GOD.** You not only get to expand your personal relationship with God, but you help to **EXPAND THE RELATIONSHIP WITH GOD** for others as well. That's the true beauty of it. That's why it's *so* important!"

Matt's eyes gleamed with belief in my message. He stood straight up tall and saluted me like a proper soldier as he said, "Okay, Ezra. That makes sense. I can do that."

I looked up with renewed confidence. "So, what about the rest of you? Are you ready to commit to doing the same?" The immediate and resounding *Yes!* I was expecting did not come. Before anyone could respond with skepticism, I added one more nugget to my proposal.

"If any of you have doubts, I want you to think of our twelve hours together in the elevator. Think of the magic that happened for all of us, both individually and together. Don't you want everyone you know to experience those same amazing feelings? And don't you think they would want to pass it on to others as well? You have the power to give everyone this amazing gift and the ability and responsibility to share this with the world. Are you ready? It's up to you now." This time I decided not to continue. I had proposed the idea and said my piece. It was now up to each of them to search inside their hearts to make a decision. I sat back down, closed my eyes, and began to pray.

CHAPTER 16: THE ANSWERS

#1

What was obvious to me may not have been for my ten new friends, although I did have faith that they would accept the challenge. I had provided them everything they needed to ignite the revolution to **CHANGE THE WORLD**. It was a big ask, a tall order, yet I knew they were up to it.

"I think I know how this is going to end ...."

Is that so, Anabeth? You've been pretty accurate so far. What do you think happened?

"I think they gave you the answer."

Yes. Anabeth, that's correct. They did give me the answer. That part is obvious, though. What do you think the answer was?

*"I think that they decided to **CHANGE THE WORLD**. I mean, I know it was centuries ago, but the world is pretty amazing today. They had to have chosen that, or else the world would be as terrible now as it was back then. I've read the history books. I know all about the abuse, poverty, anxiety, suffering, greed, pessimism, gluttony, negativity, violence, racism, and hatred of the twenty-first century. It was awful! I honestly can't comprehend how people*

lived with one another back then. Your ten friends had to have found a better way, or it wouldn't be the beautiful world of today that's filled with LOVE, PEACE, GRATITUDE, HAPPINESS, COURAGE, EQUALITY, ABUNDANCE, GENEROSITY, JUSTICE, EMPATHY, and FORGIVENESS. They definitely made the correct choice."

You may be right about that, Anabeth, but at that time I didn't get an answer from everyone right away.

As I sat there praying, I could faintly hear them discussing my proposal like a jury deliberating a verdict. I didn't want to interfere with them whatsoever, so I kept my eyes closed and concentrated on my praying.

It wasn't until sometime later that Olivia tapped me on the shoulder to let me know they were ready. She spoke for the group as if she were the jury foreman. "Ezra, first off, we all want to thank you for being courageous and ambitious enough to propose this to our group. We feel that you have had an extremely positive impact on each of us in very unique ways. Furthermore, we each feel that we will leave this elevator in a better place mentally, emotionally, and spiritually than when we entered, thanks to your guidance. We have decided to accept the responsibility to pass on what we have learned, live by the Golden Rule, and make a commitment to **CHANGE THE WORLD**."

I was nearly speechless as tears of joy streamed down my face. I exchanged hugs of gratitude with everyone and then moved back to the corner so I could address the group. "As you can see, your answer left me speechless for a few minutes, which is pretty hard to do." They all chuckled since I had basically not shut up for more than two minutes the whole time we were there. I continued, "I'm thrilled that you **HAVE FAITH** in the idea and in yourselves and that you have the **LOVE** to carry it through. I support you 100 percent and feel it's important to share a couple more things with you about the future."

"You didn't!"

No, Anabeth! I know what you're thinking. I didn't tell them about their future. Just listen and be patient.

"Sorry, Teacher! I got excited for a sec. I'll be quiet now."

Still, I had to be realistic with them. I needed to make them aware of the challenges they would face along the way. "This path that you have chosen will bring with it some challenges that you need to understand. First, making this commitment will have a significant impact on others, but it will have an incredible impact on you. If you think you've experienced change in the past twelve hours, just wait. You will experience substantially more change on a daily basis for the rest of your lives. The good news is that it will be positive change. The not-as-fortunate news is that it won't always be easy."

They all looked at one another, confirming in each other's eyes what they all felt.

"Don't worry, Ezra. Bring it on. We can all handle that bull!" touted Big John.

I laughed at the analogy. "Yes, I know you can! The second thing I need to share is that there will be people who won't accept what you offer or your beliefs. You will need to be steadfast and know that they will come around when they are ready. Remember, everything happens on God's time."

"We can handle that too, Ezra. I think our little elevator band of misfits knows a thing or two about changing when we're ready," declared Percy.

I grinned once again. "I know from first-hand experience that you are correct on that one."

They all laughed, knowing I was referring to their individual stubbornness. "Whatever happens, just know that God will always be with you, and He will always **LOVE** you. That comfort alone will be enough to carry you through any future challenges."

With that, a wave of confirmations began, one after another.

"We've got this!" asserted Matt.

"Yeah, bring it on!" Carly shouted.

"I'm excited!" exclaimed Eva.

"Me too!" added Adam.

"Game on!" Joshua announced.

"Yeehaw!" heralded Big John.

"I'm ready!" Faith cheered.

"There will be no stopping me!" yelled Olivia.

And finally, Betty added, "This old lady's gonna **CHANGE THE WORLD!**"

"*Amen!*" I bellowed. "*Amen* indeed!" It was powerful. They were on fire, truly ready in their hearts, minds, souls, and bodies.

We were so fired up that none of us noticed that the elevator had begun to move. It wasn't until a few seconds later that

Carly exclaimed, "Wait a minute! Do you all feel that? We're going down. We'll be out in no time."

With that, everyone went completely silent in anticipation and excitement. I stood in the very back, against the wall and all alone, as everyone else crammed themselves near the doors. I could faintly see the red numbers on the LED pad blinking. They were changing quickly as we passed each corresponding floor … 10, 9, 8, 7, 6, 5, 4, 3, 2, 1. With that, the doors opened to reveal a man standing outside the elevator.

"Franklin, we're so glad to see you!" shouted Big John. "Thank you for fixing the elevator and saving us!" he added.

Franklin stood there in his light blue security shirt, black hat, and accompanying safety belt and just stared at us, perplexed. "Saving you? The elevator isn't and wasn't broken. I just got here and was going up to do my rounds. When I pressed the button, it just came down." He shrugged and yelled, "Sorry! I don't know what you're talking about. I got to get moving. I'll take the service elevator instead!" as he walked off.

Everyone exchanged confused looks but hurriedly proceeded to the exit, as they had been in the elevator long enough. First Betty, then Carly, then Eva and Adam, then Matt, then Joshua, then Olivia, then Big John, and then Faith. I was about to follow when I paused to say a quick prayer. I looked up to Heaven and then closed my eyes to thank God one final time. I could faintly hear Faith's voice calling me, "Ezra, Ezra! *Where are you?*"

#2

I instantly opened my eyes to answer her but was met with an unexpected surprise. I was no longer in the elevator on Earth. I was suddenly back in the EEE with Cain's unemotional face staring at me. "How was your trip?" he asked.

I blinked, looking around. "Uh … uh … great. It was amazing, actually! Wait, how long was I gone?"

"How long? I don't know. I don't keep time on Earth trips. I just run the elevator." Cain sounded slightly annoyed.

"No, I mean, how long has it been since you told me to close my eyes when I first got in?" I questioned.

"Oh, sorry. I forgot you're a first-timer. It was only an instant. You closed your eyes, disappeared, and then you instantly reappeared again with your eyes open. That's how it always works."

"Oh … I see. It's just … I was with some people, and I didn't get to say goodbye."

Cain's stone-like stare warmed to a compassionate smile. "Don't worry, kid. I'm sure they'll remember you. You're kind of hard to forget."

I stood there, pondering what he meant.

"Here we are, kid," he announced, interrupting my thoughts. "This is where you get off."

Suddenly, I saw Barachiel standing right where I had left him on the suspended landing platform when I boarded the elevator.

"Ezra! It's so good to see you! I'm glad you're back, and not a minute too soon." Barachiel embraced me warmly like he always did, but this time it felt different. He hadn't changed, though. I had—although I couldn't exactly determine how yet.

"Hi, Barachiel," I greeted. "It's nice to be back. Have I got a story to tell you!"

He grabbed my arm as he guided me across all the corridors toward the Angel-in-Training meeting room. "Sorry, Ezra. There's no time for that right now. We have to get back. It's just about time to reconvene with all the Choirs before our final vote."

As we walked into the room, I could hear mutterings of wonder from various Angels. Most were speaking softly to one another or in small groups, though loudly enough for me to pick up most of it: "Wow, Ezra is back." "Look at him!" "I wonder what happened?" "Did he get in trouble?"

Before I could respond to anyone, Barachiel whisked me to the front of the room and got the group's attention with a pound on the stone podium. "Everyone, as you can see, Ezra has returned from a successful meeting with God. He is just in time, as we must now nominate one final Angel-in-Training to be in the running for the new Archangel. Please cast your votes now."

I remember wondering what Barachiel could be up to. And why had he brought me up to the front like this? Such behavior wasn't very typical for him, but then again, nothing he had done that day was. I didn't have time to analyze the situation. Not that it really mattered. I no longer had my previous desire to retain full control over everything. I felt completely comfortable and content.

A few short minutes later, the white parchment paper votes were tallied and handed to Barachiel, who announced, "The results are unanimous. Our Angel-in-Training Archangel nominee is … Ezra."

I automatically started clapping, then froze. *Wait! I'm the nominee?* I was flabbergasted. So much had already happened that day. This was more than I could have imagined … at that point, at least. Immediately, congratulations started to flow in from all over the room: "Way to go Ezra!" "Congrats!" "I always knew you could do it!" "You're going to do great!"

I hardly had time to thank or hug anyone before I heard Barachiel shouting from somewhere in the room, "Ezra? Ezra, It's time to return to the large group. We need to go now!" I quickly found him amongst the crowd, and we headed out as the rest of the Angels in Training followed closely behind as we made our way back to the Great Hall.

#3

Millions of Choirs of Angels were pouring back into the Great Hall from all levels and every corridor far and wide as we reached our assigned spot. We quickly sat down as Barachiel took my hand and ushered me to the front platform to board the floating stage. "This is where you are to sit, Ezra, with the other nominees." He motioned to one of the burgundy chairs with opalescent arms lined up at the front of the stage.

I sat down in my assigned spot on the massive floating stage as it began to ascend to the center of the hall, where it was surrounded by Angels in all directions. As I gathered myself I turned toward Barachiel. "Thank you, Barachiel. I have a quest—"

It was too late. He had dashed away to sit at the far back of the stage on a raised platform behind us with the seven other Archangels in their official seats of honor. I had planned to ask him what would happen next, but it didn't matter anymore. I sat there amongst some of the most senior Angels from each division and felt right at home, as if I were meant to be there. That feeling of uncertainly that was so prevalent throughout my many years of training was now gone. I felt a confidence now that was far different from the cockiness of before. It was the self-assurance of one who could teach others, a true leader.

Raphael approached the main marble podium at the front of the stage and brought the Choirs to order with a pound of his massive mighty bronze gavel. He addressed the Choirs. "The time of the hour is now upon us. We must make a selection from the final nominees. Each Choir will have three minutes to address the group and make a final case for their selection."

One by one, the candidates from each division stepped to the podium, each sharing their beliefs on everything, from what they had accomplished to why they should be chosen. All taking only the allowed three minutes to avoid the risk of being gonged from the stage. I listened intently to each candidate—a far cry from the attitude I would have displayed just a short time ago. In the past, I would have turned a situation like this into a joke. I was different now—and was beginning to realize it. I remembered Barachiel's hug as I stepped off the elevator. Every other time we had embraced I had felt a certain level of inequality, of me being lesser than him in some way. Not by his doing at all, but due to my own insecurities. These feelings had been wiped clean as if my slate had been broken and a new and improved version had been chiseled in its place.

The ninth candidate was just wrapping up her speech. It was now my time to address the Choirs. Every other candidate had simply walked up to the podium and begun to speak. They were well-known and therefore had not required any introduction. I had imagined how I would introduce myself, but it ended up not being necessary.

Raphael beat me to the podium and said, "We have now heard from the nominees from each of the Nine Choirs. However, we are not ready to cast our votes. If you recall, God has requested that all Angels, including those in training, be eligible for selection as the new Archangel."

With this reminder, a rush of laughter as thunderous as a stormy ocean moved rapidly across the crowd, sweeping everyone up in a wave of silliness, as many Angels thought it was a joke.

"Order! Order!" cried Raphael, his official purple robe beginning to glow with severity. "We will have no such behavior in our midst! We will all give the Angel-in-Training nominee our undivided and full attention." I could see the heads of each Division scolding their sections as the Choirs settled down and came to order as Raphael had requested. With that, Raphael motioned for me to come to the podium. He shook my young hand and then gave me permission to speak.

I took a few seconds to scan the vast masses of Angels,

swiveling my head until I could view every corner of the hall. An intimidating sight, to be sure, but I kept telling myself I was meant to be up there. I composed myself, said a quick prayer, and began. "Thank you, Raphael. Hello, everyone. My name is Ezra. As Raphael said, I am the newly elected nominee from the Angels In Training. The majority of you have no idea who I am, and for good reason. Up until the last twelve hours, I didn't know who I was either. If you do recognize me, it's probably because you were a recipient of one of multiple pranks I am guilty of."

Sparse laughter came from all over the hall, along with a few random shouts of acknowledgment from its farthest reaches. "That old Moses prank was hilarious!" "Oh, so you're the one!"

I cracked a slightly guilty smile and nodded. "Yes, yes. Unfortunately, those were all me. My sincerest apologies to everyone. I take full responsibility for my actions and ask for your forgiveness. Please know, however, that forgiveness is not the reason I'm up here. I actually want to share a revelation I had in the past twelve hours." I paused as the crowd settled down and waited for me to continue.

"As I said, up until twelve hours ago, I didn't know what type of Angel I was or what type I would eventually become. I only identified myself as Ezra the Jokester, the know-it-all, too smart for my own good. Always having to be in control of the situation. All of that was borne out of insecurity, as I didn't know where I fit in and was always searching for my place. For those of you who don't recall, it can be very challenging, being a newer Angel. You're always trying to follow the rules, always trying to stay ahead of your peers, and always trying to impress the higher-ups. It's incredibly daunting to someone as young as I am." I could see many affirming nods from across the room, especially the Angels In Training, who knew first-hand what I meant. "To top it all off, we are constantly told to uphold the Angelic Code of Conduct in everything we do, which is a struggle for many, many Angels, and not just the Angels in Training like me." Again, more affirming nods, and a slew of *Amens* came from around the Great Hall. I continued on, "It's time for a change, not just in new Archangel leadership but in the ACOC!"

With this, a roar of applause came from all divisions. I was clearly gaining support. I needed to say more but was running out of time. I decided to just go for it and lay it all out. "Thank you. I know that many of you will agree, the time of three tenets of the ACOC is done!" The applause increased as I paused before going for my close. "I propose we usher in the era of a new and improved *Ten-Tenet* ACOC!"

If Angels used profane language, you would have heard a collective *WTH?* from the masses staring up at me. My roaring applause had now changed to noises of dissent from far and wide. Millions of Angels from every division now jeered in opposition. What had just happened? I was doing so well, and it had all turned in an instant. Raphael stood and began to approach the podium, even though I had about a minute left. Barachiel stopped Raphael as he crossed in front of his chair by grabbing his robe and then whispered something in his ear, which caused Raphael to return to his seat. No one was going to save me. I had to save myself, which was terrifying, but I knew God was on my side.

The crowd would not settle down, so I picked up Raphael's mighty bronze gavel and slammed it down on the marble podium with a force stronger than I knew I had inside, much to everyone's surprise. I deepened my voice and shouted, "Excuse me! I believe I have some time remaining. Thank you for listening!" With that, everyone calmed down instantly, as if scolded by Michael himself. I could see Barachiel's expression, encouraging me on, so I proceeded. "Before you all pass judgment, I suggest you hear what I propose. I promise you, it will be worthwhile."

They all sat down and returned to complete silence as only Angels can. It was just then that I noticed God was watching from a cloud-enshrined balcony with His Son Jesus and the Holy Spirit at the highest and farthest ascendances of the Great Hall. It was miles off in the distance, but there was no mistaking the awe-inspiring glow and radiant love that their presence projected to me and everyone else present. It gave me instant resolve. I smiled in their direction, hoping they could feel my love before I continued. "As I was saying, it's time for a change. Both Heaven and Earth are in crises. Human beings are lost, and we're not doing much better in Heaven. Most of the people of Earth wander around from day to day living their lives in a fog. They are hurtful, selfish, prideful, loathing, distracted, entitled, negative, and unloving. There is far too much abuse, poverty, anxiety, suffering, greed, pessimism, gluttony, negativity, violence, racism, and hatred.

This is not the way God intended the world to be. He wants the absolute best for all of His children! We have not been doing a good enough job of helping them find the right direction. We need to better guide them toward LOVE, PEACE, GRATITUDE, HAPPINESS, COURAGE, EQUALITY, ABUNDANCE, GENEROSITY, JUSTICE, EMPATHY, and FORGIVENESS. We can do this by teaching them our ten new tenets of the ACOC:

1. LOVE is and always will be first, as this is the foundation for it all. Then our original core:

2. GIVE, and

3. SERVE, as these support LOVE. And now the additions,

4. SHOW GRATITUDE

5. BE PRESENT

6. GROW

7. HAVE FAITH

8. PRACTICE STILLNESS

9. FORGIVE, and the final and most important tenet,

10. EXPAND THE RELATIONSHIP WITH GOD.

With this, the room erupted in thunderous applause that dwarfed the previous laughter ten-fold. All Angels near and far were standing and cheering as loudly as their voices could muster. It was nearly deafening; I bet they could even hear it on Earth.

It was many minutes before everyone began to settle back down. Raphael approached the podium and stood next to me, patting me on the back and letting me soak it all in. It was beautiful and awe-inspiring. I instantly thanked God for what was happening. Just then, I caught another a glimpse of Him up in the balcony. He nodded at me in support. At that moment, the applause stopped instantaneously. A collective gasp came from Angels all over the hall, as they all stared straight as me. I froze, not knowing what was going on until Barachiel caught my attention. He motioned toward his back, then gestured at me to do the same. As I turned my head to look over my right shoulder, I saw them: my wings. Glorious and new, a mix of pure white like new-fallen snow and the shiniest gold from the deepest mine on Earth, glowing with a radiance and brilliance I had never seen before—and apparently, no one else had, either. I turned to look back toward God, who was beaming with the pride of a Father. He smiled, looked me straight in the eye from miles away—as only He with his power and might could do—and gave me an affectionate wink before disappearing from my sight. I felt instant **LOVE**, more powerful than I had ever felt then and to this day. It permeated throughout my entire being, beautiful and brilliant—and the memory of it is just as vivid today as it was then.

Raphael raised his hand to finally quiet everyone so he could address the Choirs. "I think it is pretty obvious who our new selection will be for the new Head Archangel. Still, we need to render a proper vote, as the decision must be unanimous. Please cast your vote now."

"Wait! Wait!" I shouted. "I have one more thing I need to share with everyone."

Raphael looked over at Michael, who nodded and pounded his staff to allow it.

"Before you cast your vote and decide whether we need change, look no further than yourself. I challenge you to ask yourself if you will **COMMIT TO CHANGE**. Ask yourself if you will **COMMIT TO MAKE A DIFFERENCE**, and ask yourself if you will **COMMIT TO MAKING GOD'S HEAVEN AND EARTH BETTER PLACES**. If you can commit to all these things today, you will not be voting for me. Rather, you will be voting for yourself and every human being on Earth from now until the end of time!" With that, I quietly returned to my seat and closed my eyes to pray, knowing God would take it from there.

#4

So ... did I answer your question, Anabeth? Are you satisfied with the answer of how I became the youngest Archangel in Heaven?

"Wow ... Wow ... Wow ... Wow! That's quite a story, Teacher. You know ... I have always wondered how you got your beautiful wings."

You're funny, Anabeth. Is there anything else you have to say?

"Yes, yes there is. First off, thank you for sharing your story with me, Teacher. I have learned a lot, and I know it will help me in the upcoming election. I'm just wondering, though, what happened with the ten people from the elevator?"

Somehow, I knew you were going to ask that question, Anabeth. If you think my story was great, you're going to absolutely **LOVE** hearing the rest of their story.

"Yes! I want to hear it! Please tell me, Teacher."

I'm sorry, Anabeth. It's getting late, and you have work to do tomorrow. We're just going to have to save that story for another day ....

So, there you have it. Hopefully, you have enjoyed my story as much as Anabeth did. Hopefully, you have a deeper understanding of what God was looking for when He asked for change. But most importantly, hopefully, it has sparked a flame inside of you that will continue to burn brightly for you and everyone you touch, both on Earth and in Heaven. Don't worry, you can do that last part from a distance for now. I'll be waiting for you when you get here.

With **LOVE**,
Ezra,

NOTE FROM THE AUTHOR

So, I make the same challenge to you that Ezra made to the ten people of the elevator.

What kind of world do you want to live in?

What kind of world do you want for your children and grandchildren and for generations to come?

Everyone complains about the world currently being in a terrible state, but no one does anything about it.

This *stops now*!

The time for *change begins with you*!

Make the commitment here and now to *change the world*!

I, (NAME) _____

_____ commit to doing my part each day to **CHANGE THE WORLD**. I promise to treat others the way I want to be treated in all that I do. I promise to practice this every day and in every way I can.

I will hold the 10 Lessons: **LOVE, GIVE, SERVE, SHOW GRATITUDE, BE PRESENT, GROW, HAVE FAITH, PRACTICE STILLNESS, FORGIVE,** and **EXPAND THE RELATIONSHIP WITH GOD** deep within my heart and share them with others.

I WILL spread this message to everyone I come into contact with in every way I possibly can and teach others what I have learned. This is *my* commitment to everyone on Earth and in Heaven.

Signed,

_____

Pick five people you want to share these lessons with and who you know are eager to **SPARK CHANGE IN THE WORLD**. Write down the five people you will give a copy of this book to:

1) _____

2) _____

3) _____

4) _____

5) _____

If this book has the impact I'm shooting for, you are probably reading it now because it was passed on by someone close to you who was personally touched by the message it contains. Or, you may have opened it because you're looking to be uplifted, or searching for hope, and you've heard such inspiration lies within. Either way, you feel that the world is not where it needs to be and there must be a better way to live.

There exists far too much abuse, poverty, anxiety, suffering, greed, pessimism, gluttony, negativity, violence, racism, and hatred throughout humanity, and these are ever-growing problems. Maybe you've felt that there's nothing you can do to improve the situation. Like most people, you're mainly focused on living the best life you can and doing all you can do to provide for your family. Or perhaps you have tried to make a difference. If so, I commend you for your courage in taking a stand.

If recent events have shown us anything, they've taught that we can all use some change in the right direction. There's an enormous need for more love, peace, kindness, gratitude, happiness, courage, generosity, service, abundance, justice, and forgiveness, among other things. Only you know in your heart and mind what you think that change should look like. Only you have the ability to make this change a reality.

In this book, I offer a glimpse of what is needed to spark change in humanity and the world. A simple guide toward change from someone who is sick and tired of everything that is happening and has taken life's challenges one day at a time. But time can pass you by before you know it, slipping away like the sands through an hourglass until you can only hope it's not too late ....

You see, this story has been in my head for twenty years. It was originally sparked after a terrible car accident in which I completely rolled my car on the highway with my wife and two young daughters on board. Through God's grace, we all miraculously escaped unharmed. It was that incident that led me to evaluate my life and think about what really mattered. In my evaluation process I wrote a "TO-DO List for every day" — a checklist of things I wanted to focus on for my family, others, and myself.

While writing that list, the idea for this book popped into my head, but I never found the time to get started. Sure, I often thought about writing it, but I didn't make it a priority. It wasn't until the COVID-19 quarantine of 2020 that I was motivated to start writing. The original spark came in the form of a blog I wrote entitled, "How to Have a Successful COVID-19 Quarantine" where I presented some recommendations on how to use this time as an opportunity to grow. Fortunately for all of us, I decided to take my own advice and finally get the story out of my head.

As I wrote over the next few months of quarantine and shutdown, the world continued to grow even worse. I used this for writing fuel, as many of the daily events of 2020 had an impact on the story and words contained herein. I wrote from my personal perspective and my beliefs based on my Catholic-Christian upbringing. This does not make this a "religious book" in my opinion, if that may scare you. It makes it a book focused on simple lessons of doing the right thing. They are referred to as Lessons for a Better World, as I feel they can have that significant of an impact. I have included some Bible verses as they relate to each lesson. You may accept the lessons however they speak to your heart.

My greatest hope is that the words and messages on these pages will resonate with some part of you and those you love. My other desire is that you will let this book, which took twenty years' worth of life to develop, impact you in the way it impacted me. I wish you well on this beautiful ride of change.

SUPPORTING SCRIPTURE

Expand the Relationship with God:

Matthew 22:37-39: Jesus said to him, "You must love the Lord your God with all your heart, with all your soul, and with all your mind. This is the greatest and the first commandment. The second resembles it: You must love your neighbor as yourself."

Matthew 6:31-33: "Do not worry then, saying, 'What will we eat?' or 'What will we drink?' or 'What will we wear for clothing?' For the Gentiles eagerly seek all these things; for your heavenly Father knows that you need all these things. But seek first His kingdom and His righteousness, and all these things will be added to you."

Matthew 6:26: "Look at the birds of the air, that they do not sow, nor reap nor gather into barns, and yet your heavenly Father feeds them. Are you not worth much more than they?"

Matthew 6:8: "Your Father knows what you need before you ask him."

John 15:16: " … the Father will give you whatever you ask in [Jesus'] name."

The Golden Rule: Do unto Others:

Matthew 7:12: "So always treat others as you would like them to treat you; that is the Law and the Prophets."

Galatians 6:10: "So then, as long as we have the opportunity let all our actions be for the good of everybody, and especially of those who belong to the household of the faith."

Forgive:

Colossians 3:13: Bearing with one another and, if one has a complaint against another, forgiving each other; as the Lord has forgiven you, so you also must forgive."

Matthew 6:14-15: "For if you forgive other people when they sin against you, your heavenly Father will also forgive you. But if you do not forgive others their sins, your Father will not forgive your sins."

Forgiveness is an act of obedience.
Mark 11:25: "And whenever you stand to pray, forgive, if you have anything against anyone, so that your Father also who is in heaven may forgive you your trespasses."

Forgiveness is an act of faith.
Matthew 18: 21-22: "Then Peter went up to him and said, 'Lord, how often must I forgive my brother if he wrongs me? As often as seven times?' Jesus answered, 'Not seven, I tell you, but seventy-seven times.'"

Forgiveness is an act of Patience. Forgiveness requires patience. Matthew 5:39-41: "But I tell you not to resist an evil person. If someone slaps you on your right cheek, turn to him the other also; if someone wants to sue you and take your tunic, let him have your cloak as well, and if someone forces you to go one mile, go with him two."
Proverbs 17:9: "Love prospers when a fault is forgiven, but dwelling on it separates close friends."

Luke 6:35-36: "But love your enemies, do good to them, and lend to them without expecting to get anything back. Then your reward will be great, and you will be children of the Most High, because he is kind to the ungrateful and wicked. Be merciful, just as your Father is merciful."

Trust:

Psalm 56:4: "In God, whose word I praise—in God I trust and am not afraid. What can mere mortals do to me?"

Proverbs 29:25: "Fear of man will prove to be a snare, but whoever trusts in the Lord is kept safe."

Romans 12:10: "Be devoted to one another in brotherly love; give preference to one another in honor."

James 1:19: "My dear brothers and sisters, be quick to listen, slow to speak and slow to get angry."

Relationships:

Ephesians 4:2-3: "Be completely humble and gentle; be patient, bearing with one another in love. Make every effort to keep the unity of the Spirit through the bond of peace."

Romans 15:5-6: "May the God of endurance and encouragement grant you to live in such harmony with one another, in accord with Christ Jesus, that together you may with one voice glorify the God and Father of our Lord Jesus Christ."

Serve:

1 Peter 10: "As each one has received a gift, use it to serve one another as good stewards of God's varied grace."

Proverbs 11:25: "Whoever brings blessing will be enriched, and one who waters will himself be watered."

Give:

Acts 20:35: "In every way I have shown you that by hard work of that sort we must help the weak, and keep in mind the words of the Lord Jesus who himself said, 'It is more blessed to give than to receive.'"

2 Corinthians 9:7: "Each of you must give as you have made up your mind, not reluctantly or under compulsion, for God loves a cheerful giver."

Proverbs 19:21: "Many are the plans in a person's heart, but it is the Lord's purpose that prevails."

Love:

John 13:34-35: "I give you a new commandment: Love one another. As I have loved you, so you must also love one another."

1 Corinthians 13:4-7: "Love is patient, love is kind. It does not envy, it does not boast, it is not proud. It does not dishonor others, it is not self-seeking, it is not easily angered, it keeps no record of wrongs. Love does not delight in evil but rejoices with the truth. It always protects, always trusts, always hopes, always perseveres."

Proverbs 3:5-6: "Trust in the Lord with all your heart, and do not lean on your own understanding. In all your ways acknowledge him, and he will make straight your paths."

Mark 12:30-32: "... and you must love the Lord your God with all your heart, with all your soul, with all your mind and with all your strength. The second is this: You must love your neighbor as yourself. There is no commandment greater than these."

Have Faith:

Romans 8:18: "The pain that you've been feeling, can't compare to the joy that's coming."

Isaiah 66:9: "I will not cause pain without allowing something new to be born, says the Lord."

Proverbs 31:25: "She is clothed in strength and dignity, and she laughs without fear of the future."

Isaiah 41:10: "Don't be afraid, for I am with you. Don't be discouraged, for I am your God. I will strengthen you and help you. I will hold you up with my victorious right hand."

Be Present:

Philippians 4:6: "Do not be anxious about anything, but in everything by prayer and supplication with thanksgiving let your requests be made known to God."

Matthew 6:34: "Therefore do not be anxious about tomorrow, for tomorrow will be anxious for itself. Sufficient for the day is its own trouble."

Grow:

John 15:5: "I am the vine; you are the branches. If you remain in me and I in you, you will bear much fruit; apart from me you can do nothing."

Colossians 1:10: "... so that you may live a life worthy of the Lord and please him in every way: bearing fruit in every good work, growing in the knowledge of God ..."

Show Gratitude:

Psalm 118:1: "Give thanks to the Lord, for he is good; his love endures forever."

Matthew 18:1-5: "He called a little child to Him and placed the child among them. And he said: 'Truly I tell you, unless you change and become like little children, you will never enter the kingdom of heaven. Therefore, whoever takes the lowly position of this child is the greatest in the kingdom of heaven. And whoever welcomes one such child in my name welcomes me.'"

ACKNOWLEDGEMENTS

Most books are the result of the work of numerous people far beyond the author, and this is definitely one of them. As a first-time author, It was only with the assistance of the following individuals that I was able to make this book a reality.

First, to my family for the love and support you have given me throughout. I am grateful for the teachings of my mother, Linda, that helped to mold me from a young age, and to my wife, Tonya, and daughters, Ciarra, Kinsey, and Hailee, who continue to shape me into a better man each day.

Hearty thanks to my business partner, Arjay Visaya, for being the best sounding board and consultant I could ever ask for in this endeavor and always. You are my brother!

To Zachary Grant, whose amazing video work provided the vehicle to spread my message around the world and to Albert Leinenweber, whose superior design skills created a logo to represent my dream.

A shout out to Darren Hardy and his Jumpstart A-Team. Your daily inspiration, books, and course all helped to nudge my writing along at just the right time.

A big thank you to all of my pre-readers, especially My success buddy, Mark Apelin; believer, Kathy Chill; colleague and friend, Tony DeRamus; listener, Estrella Godinez; advisor, Jenny Mulks; and naysayer, Laura O. van Vuuren. All of you, including those not listed here, supported me in exactly the way I needed it most.

Sincere gratitude to Andrea Vanryken for helping to make my story pop with her wonderful editing, and to Christy Collins for her fabulous design work and capturing my vision on the front cover. To my publishing consultant, Martha Bullen, who dealt with my numerous questions, frequent emails on weekends, and lack of knowledge as a newbie, you dealt with it all and held my hand through the whole process. Don't worry! I'll be back for the next book, and the next ....

To those who backed and supported my project on Kickstarter and social media — without you I would not have been able to spread the message to this point. Thank you for believing in me and what I am working to accomplish. Please keep sharing!

For Danny Bader — your mentorship of my growth as an author and inspirer has been more helpful than I could ever have imagined. You have always been there when I sought your support over the years and I know I can always count on you.

Lastly, a big thank you to everyone who is reading this book and has received inspiration. Please share it with everyone you encounter in this world. It starts with you. Be a spark for change!

ABOUT THE AUTHOR

RICK ORNELAS has had a lifelong desire to serve and has been helping others improve themselves for most of his life. He is passionate about personal development and coaches businesses and individuals in areas such as growth, communication, wellness, fitness, mental toughness and spiritual awareness. He is a lifelong learner and believes everyone has the best version of themselves ready to burst free with a little guidance.

Rick earned a bachelor's degree in Social Science-Communications from The University of Southern California. A strategic and creative thinker, he has received extensive training over the years in communication, leadership, corporate training, personality assessment, interpersonal development, fitness, and wellness.

Rick is the Founder & CEO of two companies, I Spark Change LLC and Strategic Medical Coaching, Inc. When he's not busy coaching others, wearing different hats and juggling multiple plates in the air, he enjoys spending time with his wife and three daughters. They live outside of Houston, TX.

12 Hours of Heaven: Lessons for a Better World is his first book. For more information, please visit:

www.12hoursofheaven.com
www.isparkchange.com

Praise for 12 HOURS OF HEAVEN

"*12 Hours of Heaven* is a beautiful and timely story that provides a roadmap for how we all can make the world a better place. It's an inspiring read with characters that will tug at your heartstrings and bring you joy. I highly encourage everyone to read this book and share it with others!"

— Kathy Chill, Founder & President, Chill Strategic Partners, Tech industry expert and believer & promoter of human potential

"In a world that desperately needs a positive message that is applicable to everyone, this book certainly delivers. The reader will undoubtedly be captivated from the opening chapters until the end of the book as these foundational principles of life are presented through a very entertaining and clever story of the future Archangel, Ezra. *12 Hours of Heaven* is highly recommended for anyone looking to not only make difference in their personal life, but in the lives of those around them."

— Dr. Tony DeRamus, International best-selling author of *The Secret Addiction*

"In *12 Hours of Heaven: Lessons for a Better World,* Rick Ornelas shares a timely message that has the power to move us beyond the status quo of what we see in society today. These guiding principles serve as the blueprint for creating a better world that is built upon a solid foundation of faith, love, and service."

— Mark Aspelin, author of *How to Fail at Life: Lessons for the Next Generation*

"What an amazing book! It was highly inspirational to me to begin promoting change in the world. The diversity in characters allowed me to identify myself in each one. Just like me, many readers will have the opportunity to connect with the characters in this book who reflect the everyday issues within our society."

— Estrella Godinez, BS, Clinical Mental Health Counseling MS Program at Sam Houston State University

"In its simplicity, this story contains a powerful message. As I let my rational mind go and read beyond the words, my heart was filled with inspiration and I awoke to new revelations of clear actions I could take in my life, especially toward the people in it. I encourage others to do the same with these modest, yet profound lessons and collectively, our world really will become a better place."

— Laura O. van Vuuren, MSW, LCSW, Licensed clinical social worker, author, speaker, child and family expert

"The lessons in *12 Hours of Heaven* are timeless, and the creative environment in which the characters are put together is quite engaging. I prefer books that stimulate a deep introspection for the reader, and encourage that reader to *really* look at their life, and the principles by which they practice each day. *12 Hours of Heaven* does just this."

— Danny Bader, author of *Back To Life: The Path of Resilience*